PENGUIN BOOKS
BURIAL AT SEA

Khushwant Singh is India's best-known writer and columnist. He has been founder-editor of *Yojna*, and editor of the *Illustrated Weekly of India*, the *National Herald* and the *Hindustan Times*. He is also the author of several books, which include the novels *Train to Pakistan*, *I Shall Not Hear the Nightingale*, *Delhi* and *The Company of Women*; the classic two-volume *A History of the Sikhs*; and a number of translations and non-fiction books on Sikh religion and culture, Delhi, nature and current affairs. His autobiography, *Truth, Love and a Little Malice*, was published in 2002.

Khushwant Singh was a Member of Parliament from 1980 to 1986. He was awarded the Padma Bhushan in 1974, but returned the decoration in 1984 in protest against the storming of the Golden Temple by the Indian Army.

Burial at Sea

KHUSHWANT SINGH

PENGUIN BOOKS

PENGUIN BOOKS
Published by the Penguin Group
Penguin Books India Pvt. Ltd, 11 Community Centre, Panchsheel Park,
New Delhi 110 017, India
Penguin Group (USA) Inc., 375 Hudson Street, New York,
New York 10014, USA
Penguin Group (Canada), 10 Alcorn Avenue, Toronto, Ontario,
Canada M4V 3B2 (a division of Pearson Penguin Canada Inc.)
Penguin Books Ltd, 80 Strand, London WC2R 0RL, England
Penguin Ireland, 25 St Stephen's Green, Dublin 2, Ireland
(a division of Penguin Books Ltd)
Penguin Group (Australia), 250 Camberwell Road, Camberwell,
Victoria 3124, Australia (a division of Pearson Australia Group Pty Ltd)
Penguin Group (NZ), cnr Airborne and Rosedale Roads, Albany,
Auckland 1310, New Zealand (a division of Pearson New Zealand Ltd)
Penguin Group (South Africa) (Pty) Ltd, 24 Sturdee Avenue, Rosebank,
Johannesburg 2196, South Africa

Penguin Books Ltd, Registered Offices: 80 Strand, London WC2R 0RL,
England

First published in Viking by Penguin Books India 2004
Published in Penguin Books 2005

Copyright © Khushwant Singh 2004

All rights reserved

10 9 8 7 6 5 4 3 2 1

Typeset in *Sabon* by SÜRYA, New Delhi
Printed at Chaman Offset Printers, New Delhi

To Poonam Khaira and Karan Sidhu
for the gift of friendship

1

For two days and nights his embalmed body lay in the Darbar Hall of the Governor's palatial residence overlooking the Arabian Sea. Raj Bhavan had been thrown open to the citizens so they could pay homage to the man who perhaps had done more for their country than anyone else in living memory. Though few people knew him personally, he had become a legend; the line of homage-payers bearing wreaths and flowers stretched over a mile beyond the entrance gate. Protocol had been set aside. The police merely ensured that the mourners kept moving past the bier on which he lay with a triumphant, even defiant, look on his dead face. Those who lingered, hoping to get a glimpse of his daughter and heir to his vast fortune, were disappointed. Only his ageing sisters could be seen in the hall, receiving important visitors.

In his will, published in the papers the day after he died, he had bequeathed all his property to his only child Bharati and also instructed her to have him buried at sea, close to the spot where his yacht *Jal Bharati* was usually anchored between the Gateway of India and Elephanta Island. He had spent half his life on his yacht from where he got a splendid view of Bombay's skyline without having to put up with the city's noise and foul odours, and that was where he wanted to end his final journey. He had also specifically mentioned that no religious rites were to be performed at his funeral.

Bharati was the boss of the show. She told the Governor to arrange for the gun carriage bearing her father's body to leave Raj Bhavan at 10 a.m. sharp. It would go along Marine Drive, making a ten-minute halt at Jai Bhagwan Towers, the thirty-storeyed building named after her father that was the general office of his many enterprises, so that the staff could bid their last farewell to their employer. It would then proceed towards the Gateway of India where *Jal Bharati* was anchored. Only five cars were to follow the cortege. Bharati would be alone in the first one; her aunts, their husbands and children in the next two; the fourth was for her guru and yoga teacher Swami Dhananjay Maharaj; and the last car, an open van, would carry her late father's confidante Ma Durgeshwari, a tantric god-woman, and her pet tiger Sheroo. Only Bharati, her yoga teacher, Ma Durgeshwari and Sheroo would be allowed on board the yacht.

At exactly 10 a.m. a cannon was fired from Raj Bhavan. Its boom echoed over the city. Flocks of pigeons took to their wings and wheeled around above the buildings before settling back on their perches. Thousands of crows rose in the air cawing angrily. Then silence returned. Faint notes of a military band playing the Funeral March led the procession to the bottom of Walkeshwar Hill at Chowpatty. Crowds lined both sides of Marine Drive. People stood on their balconies showering rose petals on the bier as it passed below them; women sobbed and shed silent tears for a man most of them had never seen but whose presence they had felt around them all their lives.

After the scheduled stop at Jai Bhagwan Towers, the cortege proceeded to the Gateway of India. There was a huge crowd packing the open space and the roads leading to it. Bharati stepped out of her car. She was draped in a white sari and wore dark glasses to hide her swollen eyes. The open coffin was taken off the gun carriage; six soldiers bore it on their shoulders and slowly marched through the massive gate to the yacht. Jai Bhagwan's sisters and their families bowed to the coffin and turned back like obedient orderlies. Swami Dhananjay Maharaj, tall and statuesque, clad in a white muslin lungi and a length of similar cloth wrapped round his torso, walked on beside Bharati. As did Ma Durgeshwari, in a tiger-skin skirt and a saffron silk kurta, leading Sheroo on a silver chain. As they disappeared from view the crowd broke into loud slogans: *Jai Bhagwan zindabad! Jai Bhagwan amar rahen!* (Jai Bhagwan be praised! May he be immortal!)

The small party boarded the yacht. It pulled away slowly from its mooring and headed for the open sea, grey-green under an overcast sky.

~

What transpired at the spot where Jai Bhagwan's body was lowered into the sea is known only to Bharati, Swamiji, Ma Durgeshwari, and possibly Sheroo. People made conjectures: if Jai Bhagwan did not want any religious ritual at his funeral, what were Swamiji and the tantric woman doing there?

They had heard Swamiji on their radio sets describe yoga asanas and quote shlokas from ancient Sanskrit texts. They weren't sure what he was all about. How close was he to Jai Bhagwan and Bharati? The presence of Ma Durgeshwari, leading a live tiger, was even more puzzling. Rumour had it that though Jai Bhagwan was an agnostic he had fallen to the dark charms of the tantric woman. But what could a rustic god-woman and a sophisticated tycoon have in common? The questions and conjectures grew with every passing week, and then years, but there were no clear answers.

Only the two women, the tiger and the swami knew that contrary to Jai Bhagwan's wishes, there was a prayer said for the peace of his soul and holy Ganga water sprinkled on his body before it was surrendered to the Arabian Sea. Only they knew that thereafter one of them turned away with a vow never to return to 'Bambai nagri' and the words '*Sukhi raho. Sab tumhara hai, apni bus Ganga mai aur uski yaad* (Be happy. Everything is yours; for me there's Mother Ganga and his memory).'

But of what happened in Jai Bhagwan's private cabin in the yacht minutes before his body was lowered into the sea, not even Bharati and Swamiji were aware. Bharati had kept her promise to allow

Ma Durgeshwari a private moment with Jai Bhagwan. Ma Durgeshwari shut the door behind her, approached the open coffin and stood still for a minute. Then she bent down and kissed the dead man full on his lips. Before she opened the door, she pulled out a small pair of scissors from her kurta and snipped three strands of Jai Bhagwan's sparse blue-black hair. She had something to remember him by.

~

Jai Bhagwan's memoirs published three decades earlier largely dealt with his political and social views and his plans to make India a great country. He revealed very little about his family, his friends or his emotional life. Most of what was published about these aspects of his life was based on current gossip: Why was he so reclusive? Why hadn't he ever remarried? What kind of hold did Durgeshwari have on him?

It was the same with Bharati. There were a couple of patchy biographies said to be based on interviews given by her. In none of these did she give any of her personal equations with other members of her family or her emotional relationships. She did not subscribe to any political, social or economic school of thought. Although she had been to schools in India and Switzerland, she had passed no exams and had no degrees to her credit. Whenever questioned about future plans she gave the simple answer, 'To carry on my father's legacy as best I can.' Like her father, she too was a very private person. She had inherited her good looks from her handsome father and her sickly but beautiful mother, and naturally people made conjectures of her love life. Some said she suffered from an acute father-fixation and found no man good enough to be her husband; others said she was frigid and had no desire for sex. As a matter of fact, no one really knew much about her except that she was haughty, arrogant and unforgiving towards anyone who crossed her path.

Despite these shortcomings we can fill in the gaps in our information from what people who came closest to the father and daughter had to say about them. And from some intelligent guesswork. We cannot lay claim to being authentic; at best it makes for interesting reading.

2

Jai Bhagwan's father, Krishan Lal Mattoo, wanted to bring up his only son as an English aristocrat. He often told his wife (semi-literate to him since she could only read and write Hindi) and children that in order to deal with the British, one had to speak English like them, mix with them socially as an equal, learn to eat their kind of food on expensive China using silver forks and knives, and serve them premium Scotch and vintage French wines of better quality than they could afford. Then one should tell them to their faces that it was time for them to buzz off from India and let Indians manage their own affairs.

Mattoo could afford to hold such views. He had

made a tidy fortune as a practising lawyer in the Delhi and other High Courts of India. Many a time he had confronted English barristers and got the better of them because of his grasp of the law and oratory. Indian princes, zamindars and industrialists engaged him as their counsel and paid him whatever he asked for as fees. So formidable was his reputation that people said that if you got Mattoo to appear for you, you won half the battle even before he had opened his mouth. Early in his career, Mattoo had built himself a double-storeyed mansion in Delhi's Civil Lines with an annexe for his office, a two-bedroom villa for his guests, and a spacious garden growing exotic flowers, including varieties of roses no one had seen in India before. He named it Shanti Bhavan. It was his grandest possession and he enjoyed showing it off to the rich and powerful, both Indian and English, whom he entertained as often as he could. He was a generous host. Princes of royal blood and English Governors of provinces were eager to be invited by him, for he served the best of food and wine and sometimes, as a bonus and with admirable discretion, arranged for the most cultured whores from the city's old quarter to perform mujra songs and dances for them.

Among the many people who stayed with Mattoo

whenever he was in Delhi was Mahatma Gandhi. The two men shared a special bond. Mattoo had at first been amused and faintly irritated by news of a half-naked nationalist leader come from South Africa who went about preaching non-violence, celibacy and the boycott of everything foreign. He was even said to have a fetish for fasting and enemas and personally cleaning latrines! When they first met at the house of an Indian National Congress leader in Delhi, Mattoo was prepared for self-righteous lecturing. To his immense surprise, Gandhi praised him for bringing honour and self-respect to India by worsting the British in their own law. 'Mattoo sahib, this too is fighting for freedom,' he said. Mattoo had suffered for years from a vague guilt because people who resented his success accused him of being anti-Indian and a slave to English custom. Gandhi's words came as a balm. He became an open admirer of Gandhi, though he never gave up his expensive tastes or English ways.

On one of Gandhi's visits to Delhi, Mattoo put to him his views on anglicizing his children. He expected him to have strong reservations against it. The Mahatma listened to him in silence, then said, 'I agree. We have to have some Indians who can tell the English when to get out in a language they can understand. But don't take it so far that they are ashamed of being Indian. Their roots must remain firmly embedded in Indian soil.' Mattoo was delighted. He brought his family to be blessed by Gandhi. The Mahatma took the five-year-old Jai Bhagwan in his lap and asked, 'Beta, what do you want to be when you grow up?' The boy replied without hesitation, 'Bapu, I want to become a Mahatma like you.'

The Mahatma hugged the boy close to his chest. 'You will become a bigger man than your Bapu. May Ishwara give you a long life!'

Shortly afterwards, Mattoo put in an ad in *The Times* of London: 'Wanted a nanny-governess for an Indian family comprising four children, three girls and a boy. Full board and lodging with a salary of £450 a year. Minimum stay three years. Travel fare England-India-England will be provided. Apply with credentials, references and a photograph if possible.'

Within a month over thirty applications were received. Mattoo examined each with great care and showed photographs of the applicants to his wife and children. They chose one, Valerie Bottomley, aged thirty-five. She had college education and had worked as governess in the family of a French aristocrat in his chateau near Orleans. She was now living with her parents in London, where her father, who had once been a missionary in Africa, was a vicar.

A month later Valerie Bottomley arrived in Delhi. Mattoo received her at the railway station and drove her to his mansion. The family lined up to welcome her. She looked exactly like her photograph, only more alive, of course, and in colour: auburn hair, grey eyes, a ruddy complexion, a face full of freckles. She was big-boned, brimming with good health and, Mattoo couldn't but notice, also had a large bosom and generous bottom. For some reason this seemed appropriate to him in a vicar's daughter. 'I am happy to be here,' she said in answer to their greetings. 'I know I am going to love India and I am going to love all of you.'

Valerie Bottomley's induction into the Mattoo household brought about a change in the style of living and the family equations at Shanti Bhavan. She spent the first fortnight taking stock of the situation. She was very courteous to everyone, including the servants. She addressed Mattoo as 'Sir', his wife as 'Madam'. With their consent she gave the children English names, as was common among Indian aristocracy. 'I find your names hard to pronounce,' she told them. 'Would you mind if I called you Nancy, you Ruby, you Fiona? And you, young sir, whose name I am told means 'victory', I'll call Victor.' They agreed enthusiastically and began to call each other by their English names. She taught everyone how to say 'please' before they asked for anything and 'thank you' after they had been served. The only one left out of the picture was Madam Mattoo. She refused to eat with fork and knife and continued using her fingers. She refused to rinse them in a finger bowl and went to the wash basin to wash her hands, gargle and spit water out of her mouth. Her husband told her she was becoming an embarrassment, so after some time she decided to eat her meals alone. Besides, chapattis had been replaced by slices of bread and for her a meal was not complete without a couple of hot chapattis smeared with ghee.

Valerie Bottomley took her duties seriously. While the girls were at the convent she taught Victor English, arithmetic, geography and Indian history. He had a maulvi and a pandit to teach him Urdu and Hindi. But he enjoyed neither lesson and looked forward to the next session with Valerie when she would tell him about Plato, Galileo, King Arthur and read to him from the Bible. She even showed him pictures of cars and the early aeroplanes of the time and answered his never-ending questions about

13

how they were put together as best she could. When the girls returned from school she helped them with their homework and ironed out the 'chi chi' English they spoke into propah Brit accents. She organized games for them, taught them how to play badminton and tennis. On Sundays she took them to visit the monuments of Delhi—the Red Fort, Purana Qila, Qutub Minar, Humayun's Tomb, Safdarjung's Tomb and the tombs of the Lodhi kings in Lodhi Garden. And gradually she began to feel more at home in Delhi and the Mattoo household than she had at any other place where she had worked. She was entitled to return home at the end of three years, but she did not avail of the leave due to her. Mattoo had much to be grateful for to Valerie Bottomley. She had become a member of his family and made his children as thoroughly English as he had wanted them to be.

After seeing off his clients in the evening Mattoo often went to Valerie's room to join her for a drink or two. His ambition had first taken him away from his pretty but traditional wife, and now after years of spectacular success among the British officers and westernized Indian royalty, the parting was complete. He, at least, felt no need to pretend otherwise. Valerie understood his need for relaxation and companionship after a hard day, but was tactful at first about what she offered him: good conversation, some feminine charm, some excellent Scotch that he would send across ahead of his visits. She also introduced new kinds of French vintage wines at the dinner table strictly for her and Sir. The children had fizzy drinks in Lalique cut glasses. They raised them to say 'Cheers' and 'To your good health'. Victor was happy to be treated as an adult. He adored Valerie. The girls, older than him and more sensitive to their mother's ostracism from the family circle, began to have doubts about their governess's growing closeness to their father. Between them they began referring to her as FBB—Fat Bottomed Bottomley.

In fact, it was several months after the girls had christened their governess FBB that Mattoo and Valerie became truly intimate. One evening, after a particularly busy day, Mattoo requested Valerie to make him larger drinks than usual. By his third drink he had become maudlin and was telling her how lonely he was because he had married the wrong woman. Valerie protested that he was being unfair to Madam. She also urged him to lower his voice; his family and servants should not hear him say such things. Mattoo responded by walking to the door and bolting it shut. He walked back to the sofa and dropped heavily to his knees before her. 'I am a lonely man,' he wept, 'help me.' Because Valerie's heart went out to him, she unbuttoned her blouse. Her breasts spilled out and a grateful Mattoo buried his face in them with a sigh. 'The family will begin to wonder; we don't have much time,' Valerie whispered. Pleased with her eagerness, Mattoo sat back and commanded her to strip and bend over before him. She did, offering him her generous buttocks. Mattoo grunted softly to express his delight. He went up on his knees again and entered her from behind. 'It will be faster this way,' he said. 'You are a savage, sir,' the missionary's daughter giggled, and Mattoo heaved into her with schoolboy impatience. At forty he had finally realized a childhood fantasy— to fuck a white woman, a gori mem.

~

Five more years went by. Jai Bhagwan, Victor to everyone including himself, looked every bit the son of an English county gentleman: cravat, waistcoat, striped trousers. And impeccable manners. 'I want him to go to the best public school in England, then Oxford or Cambridge and the Inns of Court,' said Mattoo to Valerie one evening. 'How does one go about it?'

Valerie thought over the matter before she replied:

'There are lots of excellent public schools in England. There are Eton and Harrow, of course. Equally good are Rugby, Winchester, St Pauls, Hailbury and some others. I could write to them on your behalf and get application forms. A reference from an alumni in a good position would be a great help. I am sure the Viceroy and Governors of some provinces are products of one or the other of these schools. You must know some of them.'

'No problem,' replied Mattoo. 'You get the application forms, I'll do the rest.'

It was easier than Mattoo had apprehended. On legal business in Allahabad he called on the Governor and told him of his plans for his son. 'Jolly good idea,' replied the Governor who turned out to be an Etonian. 'The best place in the world to knock fancy notions out of a lad and turn him into a worthy gentleman. I'll write to the headmaster about him. What did you say his name is?'

'Jai Bhagwan Mattoo. He's been schooled at home by an English governess of the name of Miss Valerie Bottomley. A most worthy lady, if I may say so. An English public school is *her* idea. She's given my son an English name, Victor, after Jai Bhagwan.'

The Governor made a note on a slip of paper. 'I shall send across a letter, attach it to the boy's form for admission.' After a pause he added, 'If I were you I would drop the Mattoo part of his name while he is in England. Victor J.B. would be easier for him. Next time you are in Allahabad bring the boy with you. I'd like to give him a dekho.'

Mattoo returned to Allahabad a week later, taking his son and Valerie Bottomley in tow. All three were invited to tea by the Governor's wife. Victor had been coached how to address his host and hostess. His manners, as always, were impeccable. 'How kind of you to invite me, Your Excellency,' he said to the Governor's wife as he put out his hand to shake hers. Valerie curtsied to both of them and did not open her mouth till she was questioned. The Governor asked Victor a couple of questions. 'How old are you, young man?'

'I will be thirteen next birthday, Your excellency.'

'Good, good. And what do you plan to become? India's leading lawyer or judge of a High Court?'

'I haven't yet made up my mind, Your Excellency. My father would like me to take over his practice but I want to make things like railway engines, cars and trucks. I think India needs those things more than lawyers.'

Everyone laughed. 'You are absolutely right,' said the Governor. 'Don't mind my saying so in front of your father, but lawyers are an absolute nuisance.' There was another round of laughter. The Governor turned to Valerie Bottomley. 'I don't think he need go to a prep school, do you Miss Bottomley?'

'No, Your Excellency. I've taken him over all the subjects they teach in prep schools. He's old enough to join any public school. And bright as they come.'

'I'm sure. The little I've seen of him, you've done a good job.'

'Thank you, Your Excellency.'

A second letter to the Head Master of Eton followed: the boy had been interviewed by a distinguished Etonian. That settled the matter—Master Victor J.B. could join school beginning of the Michaelmas term.

Mattoo wrote to Gandhi telling him of his son's admission to Eton and asking him for his blessings. Gandhi replied on a postcard approving of his decision. 'We must get the best we can out of the English to enable us to fight them on equal terms. But as I have said before, our roots must remain embedded in our Indian soil,' he wrote. 'If I happen to be in Bombay, which I often am, tell Jai to see me and receive my blessings for whatever they are worth. I may be a Mahatma in the eyes of others, I am Bapu Gandhi to him.'

Mattoo showed the letter to his daughters and read it out to his wife. They felt terribly proud of Victor; he was the favoured child of Bapu Gandhi! They were all in awe of the Mahatma: Mrs Mattoo had taken to spinning the charkha for an hour every afternoon; the girls had taken to wearing handspun khadi. Mattoo made no such compromises with his style and comfort but continued to be Gandhi's greatest admirer. Valerie Bottomley too became conscious of being the mentor-guide of a boy who would be equally British and Indian of the highest order. Some weeks before his departure she asked Victor to write an essay on 'The India of My Dreams' that she could send to Gandhi before they met in Bombay.

Victor was a serious-minded young lad, but he had not yet thought much about what he would like the India of the future to be. His mind was usually too full of the deeds of Alexander and Napoleon and images of cars and machines that he never saw in his country. He had vague notions of what Gandhi had in mind; he asked his father to explain it in detail. His father gave him a few reference books to read. 'Don't be influenced by what Gandhi or anyone else has to say. Try and make up your own mind,' Mattoo advised him.

Victor went about the task with a zeal no one expected from a boy of thirteen. He made notes, made drafts, tore them up and started all over again. He questioned his father, sisters, mother and his governess. 'Cocky little prig; he thinks he is about to draft the Constitution of modern India,' remarked his eldest sister one morning. Victor ignored her sarcasm.

After a fortnight Victor had his final draft ready. His essay began with a quote: 'I see a great nation poised as in a dream—waiting for the word by which it may live again.'

'Where did you get that from?' asked Valerie Bottomley.

'From someone called Edward Carpenter. I liked it.'

'Then you must say who said it. You must not take credit for something said by another person.'

Victor felt snubbed. 'Very well. I'll acknowledge his words,' he said.

Valerie went on to read what he had to say. He contradicted everything Gandhi stood for: handspun cloth, self-sufficient villages, very basic education. Victor wanted to see an India which had modern textile mills, steel plants, automobile factories, huge dams and thousands of miles of canals, every village connected by road, more schools, colleges and hospitals. In short, the most prosperous country in the world, free of religious and caste prejudices, etc., etc. He ended his essay with the Latin phrase '*Novus Ordo Seclorum*'—'new order for the ages'.

Valerie smiled to herself. The boy was a bit of a show off. She had taught him some Latin but was not familiar with this motto. 'And where did you get this from?' she asked.

'American Constitution,' he replied smugly.

'I don't think the old man will like your views,' said Valerie. 'You better let your father take a look at it.'

Mattoo read his son's essay many times. He had several copies made of it, posted one to Gandhi, one to the Governor of the United Provinces, and others he gave to friends. Everyone sent back notes of appreciation. 'If he can write this kind of essay at thirteen,' wrote the Governor, 'he will go a long way.' Mattoo had no doubt his son would go places but was still a little apprehensive about how Gandhi would react to his ideas.

Some weeks later Victor and Valerie Bottomley took the Frontier Mail for Bombay. They were given a grand farewell at the Delhi railway station. All Mattoo's relations and friends were there with garlands. Even the family priest who had some reservations about Brahmins going overseas said prayers to absolve the boy of the sin of crossing the dark waters. Victor's mother and sisters could not hold back their tears. His father kept a straight face and simply said: 'Send me a cable when you get to England. And don't forget to ring up every Sunday to give us your news.'

Valerie Bottomley was accompanying Victor to see him settle in Eton and take the leave due to her. She quietly bade farewell to members of the Mattoo family and got into the first-class coupe reserved for them. As the train pulled out of the station she noticed Victor had tears in his eyes. He was not an emotional boy, but taking leave of his family he would not see for some years was a bit too much for him. He took off the garlands round his neck and put them on the table, then sat quietly at the window watching the countryside. It was an express train; it did not stop at Mathura, halted a brief five minutes at Agra and sped on its way to Bombay. Valerie did not disturb him. They sat in silence till it was time for lunch. She opened the hamper Mrs Mattoo had packed for them and laid out small plates, forks and knives.

'Cheer up lad!' she said jovially. 'You are going

to have a wonderful time in Old Blighty. Sons of the best of English society at school to play with; pretty English girls to flirt with while you are on vacation in London. I will find you a nice flat in some mews near Hyde Park where you can entertain your friends. Enjoy yourself. Travel round the country and Europe. I know you will love it.'

Victor knew he would. He had dreamt about it for months now. He had collected pictures of Eton, Windsor Castle, London, Oxford, Cambridge, the New Forest, the Cotswolds, the Midlands—all very picturesque. Also of ballet dancers and pretty English girls on horseback and bicycles. They had stirred in him a desire to get to know them. But there was still a heaviness in his heart and he ate in silence, waiting for the sadness to go away. He was not familiar with this feeling. He did not know how to deal with it.

They dozed after lunch, saw more of the countryside through which they were passing and by late afternoon Victor was feeling lighter. They had cheerful conversation at dinner before they rested for the night. Next morning the train pulled up at Bombay's Victoria Terminus. One of Mattoo's industrialist friends had sent his secretary to meet them and bring them to his home on Malabar Hill. They were to spend two days in Bombay before boarding a PO steamer, the *Strathclyde*, bound for Southampton.

Victor had never seen the sea before. He gaped with wide-eyed wonder at the vast expanse of water on the drive along Marine Drive. His room on the Malabar Hill mansion gave a splendid view of the Arabian Sea. That this vast expanse of water was also part of India made him suddenly and unaccountably proud of his country. Everything seemed possible here. That morning he made a deep connection with the sea that was to grow stronger as the years passed.

Valerie and he joined their host, hostess and their family of several sons and daughters at lunch. It was Gujarati vegetarian fare served in silver thaalis and katoris. They had to use their fingers and it was clumsy business but their hosts did not appear to notice. The family were overawed by the handsome Kashmiri boy's stature and the fact that he was going to the very best public school in England. They were even more impressed when their father announced that Gandhi had come all the way from his ashram in Gujarat to meet the boy. He was to call on the Mahatma next morning at 11 a.m. sharp (Gandhi was very fussy about punctuality, they all knew) at the house of another industrialist where he was staying. It was only a few minutes' drive but he must be sure to be there on the dot of time.

Victor went to see Gandhi by himself. He was shown to the large room occupied by the great man. He was sitting on the floor writing replies to letters on postcards stacked by his side. As Victor entered, he told his secretary they were not to be disturbed for the next half hour. 'Come beta, sit in front of me; it is not very comfortable on the floor but that is what most of our countrymen and women sit and sleep on.' Victor felt an instant calm in Gandhi's presence; he had the warm, soft scent of his mother. Gandhi had Victor's article by his side. 'I've read all you have written here very carefully. You don't seem to approve of my idea of what we should make of India. You want to see India become westernized and full of material goods. You may have a point there as most Indians might want to become rich, live in big houses, have motor cars, wear fancy clothes. I am sure they will achieve these material ambitions but in the process lose their souls and their Indianness.'

'Bapu, I don't understand souls,' interrupted Victor.

Gandhi smiled and asked, 'Do you believe in God?'

'I am not sure,' replied Victor. 'I have never seen him.'

'You believe in truth?'

'I do. That is why I wanted you to read my essay. I feared you would not like what I have written, but it comes from my heart; it is the truth as I see it.'

'If you believe in truth you believe in God. There is nothing more to be said on the subject,' Gandhi said and put a hand on Victor's head to bless him. 'So you are going to Eton and then Oxford. You could not do better. Also join the Inns of Court and become a barrister. I was at the Inner Temple. I became a barrister but I gave up legal practice after a few years. I felt there were more important things to do than earn a living off other people's quarrels. Don't you agree?'

'I do. But I want to stand on my own feet before I put my ideas into practice.'

'You have my blessings. Write to me whenever you feel like it. My answers may be brief but I answer every letter I can. May God be with you.'

It was a brief ten-minute interview. Victor touched Gandhi's feet and left—elated as anyone would be after receiving a saint's benediction.

Valerie and Victor spent the next day driving around Bombay. They went to see the Elephanta Caves and ate their meals at the Taj: neither could stomach the Gujarati vegetarian food their hosts served. 'There is nothing Indian about the city except the people,' remarked Victor as they emerged from the Taj after dinner. 'All the big buildings are of British design. The only genuinely Indian structure is Elephanta and that is a couple of miles offshore.' Valerie wasn't sure if this was a complaint or merely an observation and decided not to respond.

The day following, their host accompanied them to the docks where the *Strathclyde* was anchored. There were two gangways, one for first-class passengers, the other for economy class and porters. There were barely two dozen whites on the first-class gangway; Victor was the only Indian. The other gangway was crammed with Indians and porters carrying their baggage. Valerie and Victor took leave of their host and went up to the deck where they were met by the bursar who escorted them to their cabins alongside each other. An hour later the *Strathclyde*'s sirens boomed across the city; it was unfastened from its moorings and gently glided out into the open sea. Victor watched the Bombay skyline recede into the distance. It would be some years before he saw India again. His voyage of the discovery of the new world had begun.

3

It was mid-September but the aftermath of the monsoons still made the sea turbulent. Valerie and Victor were given a table for two but before they could get to the second course of their lunch, Victor asked to be excused and went back to his cabin to lie down on his bunker. About an hour later Valerie brought him some fruit and bread rolls. 'Are you all right, Victor? You better have something to eat,' she said putting the plate on his side table. 'Just a little queasy in the stomach,' replied Victor. 'Not used to the rocking and rolling. Don't worry, I'll get the better of it soon.'

Victor didn't touch the bread or the fruit, nor joined Valerie for tea. He just lay flat on his back and was angry with himself. 'If Valerie and the other whites can take the pitching and rocking in their stride, why can't I?' The years of sheltered, privileged upbringing had bred in him an easy pride; he hated to be seen as awkward and out of his element.

In the evening he willed himself to get up, changed into a dinner jacket his father had got tailored for him and went out on the deck to take a stroll. There were very few people about. He strode up and down the deck, watching the sun go down under the soupy-grey waters. As the dinner gong was sounded he was at his seat in the dining room. Valerie joined him shortly afterwards. She had put on a long black dress and looked more lovely than she ever had in all the years Victor had known her. 'I've been looking for you everywhere, you were not in your cabin nor in the bar. What were you up to?'

'Working up an appetite for dinner,' Victor replied with a warm smile. 'I walked round and round the deck till I got used to the ship's see-sawing. Now I can enjoy my dinner.'

And so he did. The band struck up dance music: foxtrot, samba, waltzes. Three couples took the floor. Valerie hauled Victor from his chair and said, 'Come lad, you must learn to dance or you'll be left out of social life in England.'

Victor obeyed. He watched her steps, then his own. He moved a little clumsily at first but soon got the hang of it. 'By the time we get to Southampton you'll be an excellent dancer,' Valerie assured him.

All went smoothly for the next few days. He played deck tennis, bingo, tambola and other games organized by the bursar. One evening while he was waiting for Valerie to join him at dinner, he sensed the Australian couple at the next table were talking about him.

'Andsome nigger, ain't 'ee,' said the middle-aged woman.

'Sush! You mustn't use bad language,' said her husband sharply. Victor's face flushed with anger but he kept his cool.

'I said 'andsome, dinn I?' protested the woman. 'Ee must be a prince or raja; the white woman with him is his governess. That I found out.'

This made Victor feel better, but he decided he would be coolly hostile towards them anyway. Oddly enough it was the same Australian couple who went out of their way to befriend Valerie and him. The woman who had called him 'nigger' took the lead. 'Pardon me,' she said coming up to their table, 'why don't you two join us? Don't you get tired of talking to each other?' So their tables were joined and the

31

Australians ordered a bottle of French champagne to celebrate the occasion. 'Mind you, we 'ave good wines back 'ome but these Pommies get the cheapest and the worst to serve on their boats. Mean bastards.'

Mrs Australian had Victor next to her. As her husband poured out the champagne, she lit a cigarette. Victor had never seen a woman smoke and watched her with greater curiosity than he would have preferred to betray. He was fascinated by the sight of her scarlet lips and nails. Victor's poorly disguised interest in her amused the lady, and soon she had a hand resting on his thigh under the table, her long nails grazing his balls. Victor stiffened, but pretended nonchalance. 'So it's Eton you're going to, eh?' she asked. 'I'll bet you could speak better English than they; I love your British accent. But *don't you* become a snob like them, stay a 'andsome darkee prince and teach them a thing or two 'ow to behave.' Dinner arrived soon afterwards and with a gentle squeeze the lady withdrew her hand from Victor's thigh. That night Victor dreamt of Mrs Australian, bare-breasted and smelling of over-ripe fruit. She was sitting by his bed, smoking an enormous cigarette and massaging his thighs. It was his first wet dream and he was alarmed by it. The next day, he avoided the Australian couple, but by evening they were sharing tables again. To Victor's relief, the lady kept her hands to herself and entertained them with stories of her last sea voyage, from Australia to Japan.

By the time the *Strathclyde* dropped anchor at Aden they were on the best of terms. As advised by Valerie none of them went on shore. 'There's nothing to see—only rows of little stores run by Indians. And skinny Arab beggars who chew qat all day long to kill their appetites and get high on the weed.' They should wait till the ship steamed into the Red Sea, she said; 'It will be magical.' And it was. The sea was as placid as a lake, with dolphins gambolling about the ship as it glided over the water. There were moonlit nights, drinking and dancing on the open deck. It would stay in Victor's memory for years to come.

The Australians had booked themselves to get off at Ismailia, see the pyramids and the Sphinx and re-board the ship at Port Said. Valerie had overlooked doing that, or perhaps deliberately not chosen to do so. 'I'd rather see those places in picture books than go with those horrid Egyptian guides. They hate us English and they fleece every tourist of his last penny,' she told Victor by way of apology. 'You will enjoy going through the Suez Canal and see what the British did for the ungrateful wretches.'

'It was the French engineer De Lesseps who laid the canal, not the British,' Victor corrected her.

'Ah yes, but with British money,' she retorted. 'It is the British who keep ships moving through it. You will see the pilots who take over and steer them through the seventy-two-mile narrow canal are English, not French or Egyptian. Fat lot of gratitude they get for it!'

The journey through the canal was indeed memorable. Though he did not acknowledge it to her, Victor was full of admiration for the English pilots. A long line of ships snaked their way through the canal so narrow that at times you could not see the water below unless you leaned over the railings. Victor remembered reading in one of the journals his father received from a Congress leader that thousands of Indian soldiers had been sent to secure the Suez Canal for the British against the Turks during the Great War. He thought of telling Valerie that but then changed his mind. He was quiet as they passed through a brown desert stretching endlessly on either side: a few nondescript habitations with groves of date palms, and dust everywhere. A few hours later the ship docked at Port Said. It was to stay there for eight hours for refuelling and taking on fresh provisions. Passengers were allowed to go on land but warned to be back on board an hour before sailing.

Valerie warned Victor. 'Don't buy anything from the peddlers. They are cheats and vagabonds. If you want anything there is a big department store, SIMON ARTZ, with fixed prices. If I were you, I should have a look at the De Lesseps statue—it's a long walk with the sea on either side. We can have a nice cup of tea in a respectable hotel afterwards and get back in good time.'

Valerie was right: no sooner had they got down the gangway than they were surrounded by peddlers in jabellas selling dates and chocolates in beautifully packed boxes. They were joined by sellers of picture postcards with explicit portrayals of men and women copulating with each other and with dogs and horses. Victor was aghast and decided to protect his governess from the uncouth men. Before he could speak, though, Valerie had taken charge. She had clearly experienced this onslaught before and waved her hands about firmly, trying to shoo them off, first politely—'We don't want to buy anything, please leave us alone'—then rudely—'Bugger off!' Victor had never heard her use the word before.

'*You* bugger off,' retorted a postcard-seller. 'You fat-bottomed bitch.'

'Disgusting!' said Valerie, her face flushed red.

'One word more and I'll smash your teeth in,' shouted Victor angrily.

The postcard-seller guffawed. '*You* smash my teeth? You black Indian toady. Come, I show you both what I have,' he said with a leer, pointing to his dick and thrusting his pelvis at them.

Valerie had had enough. She pushed past the man with surprising force, and Victor followed. At last they shook off the peddlers and proceeded on their walk on the long causeway to the De Lesseps statue. They were in no mood to talk. And instead of having tea in some restaurant, decided to return to their ship. Valerie got her own back on Egypt. Passengers who had got back before them or stayed on board were bargaining for goods hauled up in baskets from peddlers on land. 'Don't buy a thing,' she went around telling everyone. 'It will be nice dates or chocolates on the top and a layer of sawdust beneath. I've been here before. Take my word for it.' Nobody bought anything and baskets full of wares were let down as they had come up. A torrent of abuse rose from the peddlers below. An Egyptian magician, the gilli-gilli man, was allowed on board. He produced broods of fluffy yellow chicks out of his fez cap. Everyone applauded; everyone gave a little bakshish. Valerie turned up her nose. 'It's cruelty on those poor little chicks. They'll all be dead by tomorrow. You take it from me.' She breathed a sigh of relief when the siren for departure was sounded and the gangplanks taken away.

'Valerie, you don't seem to like Egyptians,' said Victor gently when they met for dinner.

'But they are detestable! Didn't you see what happened out there?' He had, but he was certain some Indian men would also have behaved in that manner in similar circumstances. So did she think Indians detestable too? He put the thought out of his mind.

The Australian family had a different story to tell. They had enjoyed their visit to the pyramids and the Sphinx and were full of praise for the guides. 'Oldest civilization in the world,' bubbled Mrs Australian. 'Our guides were so polite, cultured and good looking. Older the civilization, more civilized their men, if you ask me.' Valerie pretended she had not heard her. 'Let's enjoy our dinner,' she said. 'We are now in the Mediterranean, with more cultured people inhabiting its northern shores—Greeks, Italians, French, Spaniards.' Mrs Australian thought that funny for some reason and chortled merrily. 'Horrid Arab men got to 'er,' she said and winked at

Victor. To his surprise, he found himself winking right back! He felt light and easy and very grown up.

It was through the Mediterranean after that, bluer than all the seas they had traversed. Then round the Cape of Gibraltar towards the English Channel. The ship glided into Southampton. They bade goodbye to the Australians and took the boat train to London.

4

Reverend Thomas Bottomley was vicar of the Anglican Church of Harrow-on-the-Hill. 'If you were at Harrow instead of Eton it would have been easier for everyone. You could spend weekends with us in the vicarage,' he said to Victor. 'Eton is a good distance from us. I'll drive you up the day you have to join.'

The vicarage was next to the church. On the other side was a small graveyard where parishioners who had passed away slept amidst ancient cypress and yew trees. The church was well removed from the main road which led to the school and came alive only on Sundays for the morning and evening service. The rest of the time it was as quiet as the adjacent cemetery. The vicarage was a small cottage with three bedrooms, a sitting-dining room and a study. Valerie and her two sisters had to share one bedroom; Victor had one to himself. He spent the first afternoon writing to his parents—to his father in English, giving an account of the voyage and how the Egyptians disliked British dominance; to his mother in Hindi, telling her of the people he had met and how nice Valerie's family was to him. One of Valerie's sisters accompanied him to the nearest post office from where Victor sent a telegram to his father announcing his safe arrival in England.

Victor joined the family at dinner—a special turkey dinner for Thanksgiving for Valerie's return home. Before the meal, they lowered their heads and said grace. It was a happy family reunion. Victor was charmed by it. Valerie's father opened a bottle of port wine; every one took a couple of glasses each. Victor joined them, sipping his wine while Reverend Bottomley recounted stories about his time as a young missionary in Africa.

The next day was a Sunday. Victor accompanied the family to the morning service. While in Delhi Valerie always went to St James's Church in Kashmiri Gate and attended the midnight mass and Christmas Eve, but never asked Victor or any other member of the Mattoo family to come with her. For the first time Victor saw the inside of a church, heard the congregation sing and Reverend Bottomley preach sermon. None of it moved him; only added to his information about what went on inside a church.

The following day Valerie took Victor in a bus to Harrods on Knightsbridge. She bought him a camel-hair dressing gown, woollen socks, a raincoat and an umbrella. His school uniform and the top hat Etonians wore would be purchased from the school store.

The third day, Valerie and her sisters took Victor for sightseeing. They sat on the upper deck of a tourist bus which took them round London's main tourist attractions: Buckingham Palace, Houses of Parliament, Westminster Abbey, Trafalgar Square, St Paul's Cathedral, Tower of London, British Museum and the Tate Gallery. They had sandwiches to munch whenever hungry and had tea in Kew Gardens. It was a long, tiring day. 'I didn't get to see many of these places while I lived in London. Thank you, Victor. Now I can tell your family about them.'

This was the first time Valerie had mentioned her plans to return to India. 'You're going back again?' asked one of her sisters in surprise. 'We thought you'd come back for good, to get married and settle down.'

Valerie laughed. 'I have taken three months' leave from duty. I still have Victor's sisters to teach and parents to look after. They are my responsibility.'

'Don't think Mum and Dad will like that. Have you told them?'

'I will by and by. I'll be living on my own mostly. Victor's father wants him to have a small flat in central London where he can stay during his vacations. I'll look for one around Mayfair or Marble Arch near Hyde Park or Kensington Garden. I'll stay there till I return.'

Valerie's sisters told their parents. They were disappointed. 'It's her life; she'll do what she likes,' said her mother. 'If she likes being in India rather than in England, so be it.' Reverend Bottomley made no comment. He knew his daughter well enough to suspect that it wasn't India that had claimed her loyalty—by her own admission she hadn't seen much of it. It had to be something else, but he preferred not to probe.

Within days Valerie had found a tiny mews apartment behind Albion Street: one-bed-sitter, kitchenette and loo-cum-shower. The rent was reasonable. She signed a six-year lease in her own name. In that area owners were reluctant to let their premises to coloured people. Who their white tenants entertained or sublet their premises to was no longer their business. Valerie took Victor to see it. He fell in love with it for its snug cosiness. One electric radiator warmed the whole flat. Valerie took him around to show him where he could get his bread, butter, cheese and groceries. She took him to the Speaker's Corner where they heard speakers extolling the greatness of God as well as Communists spewing lava against the church and British Imperialism. 'It is a great institution, this,' Valerie explained to Victor. 'You let off steam on any subject you like and nobody gives a damn. It is a free country, with freedom to say what you like or dislike.'

'We don't see this freedom in India,' Victor said to her and laughed. 'You mustn't be cheeky,' Valerie reproved him, though she was smiling. Nothing more was said on the subject since they both disliked arguments and in any case, neither saw the other as English or Indian.

In the evening they walked down Bayswater Road to Notting Hill Gate. There were lots of painted women standing or walking along the footpaths. Even thirteen-year-old Victor could tell they were up to no good. 'Don't ever, ever stop to talk to any of these hussies, they are the lowest of the low,' Valerie warned him. Victor promised that he would not.

Three days later Rev. Bottomley and Valerie accompanied Victor to deliver him into the hands of the headaster of Eton. They received a cordial welcome. 'I am sure he will be happy here,' assured the headmaster. 'We will take good care of him.' He showed them round the school and the dormitory he was to share with five other boys. They were putting their clothes and books in cupboards. The headmaster introduced Victor to them. His things were dumped on his bed. 'I think we should leave him here to get to know his room mates,' said the headmaster. Rev. Bottomley shook hands with Victor; Valerie kissed him on both his cheeks and turned away, overcome with emotion.

The boys who had stood to attention while the headmaster was there, relaxed. 'So you are Victor. What kind of Indian name is that?' asked the biggest of the five.

'My full name is Victor Jai Bhagwan. Victor for short,' he replied.

'Very well, Victor-for-Short, you are going to be my fag,' said the big boy. 'You will press my clothes, polish my shoes and do as I tell you.'

Valerie had warned Victor about fagging and been uncharacteristically frank about it. Victor, in fact, had practised his response in several imagined scenarios even before they had left India. 'Yes sir,' he now replied with a bow. 'We've been polishing Englishmen's shoes in India for over a hundred years. I'll be happy to polish yours in England.'

'Smarty, ain't ee?' sneered the big boy, then added. 'There may be some buggery too, if you don't mind.'

'Not at all, sir; the English have got us accustomed to that practice as well. They are also getting used to being buggered by Indians,' replied Victor.

That short dialogue put an end to Victor's fagging. A few days later, Victor was polishing the big boy's shoes, the big boy was polishing Victor's. There was no attempt at buggery. They took their shower together without as much as looking at each other's pubic hair.

Victor had no problems adjusting to life in Eton. He was among the first three or four boys in his form in every subject, including Latin. Although not familiar with slang his command over classical English was better than theirs. He did not relish outdoor life because he found the climate too cold and damp for his liking. Dutifully he took part in all the school sports without enjoying any of them. He was happier sitting in the warm library and poring over pages of newspapers and magazines.

Came December and the boys began to make plans to join their families for Christmas. The big fellow wanted Victor to spend it with his family in their country house in Suffolk. Valerie wanted him to spend it with her parents in Harrow-on-the-Hill. Victor politely turned down both invitations and asked Valerie if he could spend Christmas on his own in Albion Mews while she was with her family. 'Christmas alone?' she asked. 'You are an odd creature. However, I'll leave you some turkey and Christmas pudding. Just heat them up and open a bottle of port wine. There'll be a nice Christmas carols programme from Kings College chapel on the BBC. You'll enjoy that.'

Three days before Christmas Victor took the morning bus for central London. It dropped him off at Marble Arch, a five-minute walk from Albion Mews. Valerie awaited his arrival. She had done up the flat with coloured buntings, balloons and a miniature Christmas tree lit up with tiny bulbs. She had prepared hot lunch for him. They put in a call to Delhi. Victor spoke to his parents and sisters and told them he was in good shape and enjoying himself.

'Sure you won't change your mind and come with me to Harrow? Sure you want to be by yourself on your first Christmas in England?' asked Valerie as she cleared the lunch things, washed the plates and put them in their place.

'Quite sure,' replied Victor. 'I'll stroll round London and see how others enjoy themselves.'

'You won't find many people on the streets. Good people will be with their families. There'll be lots of drunks in the pubs. Be careful crossing roads.'

'I'll look after myself, don't worry,' replied Victor. 'I have to be back in school after Boxing Day.'

'And I'll be back here the same evening. Merry Christmas and do look after yourself,' she said as she kissed him on both cheeks. She picked up her small valise and parcels of gifts for her family and left.

Victor stretched himself in the armchair. It was wonderful to be alone and away from the noise of traffic and small talk. He had nothing against people, he liked them well enough. But sometimes they tired him, because for as long as he could remember, he had felt superior to others. He was special, he knew it in his bones; he had known it ever since he was five and Bapu Gandhi had sat him on his knee and predicted that he was destined for greatness. It was when he was alone that he felt this most strongly. That Christmas at Albion Mews was the beginning of a pattern of regular periods of solitude that would mark the rest of his life.

He decided to take a short snooze before he stepped out. Beneath his pillow he found a small packet tied in a red ribbon with a card depicting a red robin and holly leaves. It read: 'Merry Christmas and love from Val.' He opened it. It contained a silk tie with blue and white stripes and a silk handkerchief to go with it. It struck him that he should have also given her a Christmas present. He decided to get one for her for the New Year.

Later in the evening he went out to see what was going on at the Speaker's Corner. It was deserted. He walked along Oxford Street. All the stores were brightly lit up with Father Christmases and their reindeer sleighs. They were crammed with people doing their last-minute Christmas shopping. He turned into Regent Street. It was the same but with fewer people. Piccadilly Circus was again crowded with young men and women sitting round Eros Statue. He turned towards Leicester Square and found Gerard Street. He had been told it had the only two Indian restaurants in London. He went past several painted women Valerie had warned him about. A few propositioned him: 'Like a good time, dearie?'; 'Give you Christmas concession. Only five pounds.' He ignored them. He found the big Indian restaurant Koh-i-Noor and entered it. The smell of stale curry and spices assaulted his nostrils. He had not smelt Indian food for some months.

He took his seat and examined the menu. Every item was highly priced. He chose chapattis, daal and lamb curry. The Indian waiters took his order without a smile. He wasn't much of a customer. This angered him and he wished he had fistfuls of money to throw in their faces. There were very few diners: two Indian families gobbling food with their fingers, and a couple of Englishmen still drinking their Scotch and soda and nibbling 'pappadams'. The atmosphere was dingy. Victor relished the food only because it was Indian. There were a variety of chutneys and pickles on the table. He spiced his daal with them and decided it was worth the money.

He walked back the way he had come. The shops had put up their shutters. It had turned cold; there were fewer people on the streets. Only prostitutes lolled about their beats hoping for customers so they too could get a hot meal somewhere.

On Christmas Day London was strangely quiet. Hardly any sound of traffic. Church bells tolled. It was a bright sunny morning. Victor took a walk in Hyde Park. There were few people about. Silence pervaded over Speaker's Corner. The only sign of activity he noticed was men and women on horseback trotting along Rotten Row. It was a long two-hour walk in the crisp, cool air in what was aptly called the lungs of London. By the time he crossed over Bayswater to Albion Street he was tired and hungry. As soon as he was in his flat he switched on the gas stove and put a plateful of turkey in the oven. While it was being heated he uncorked the bottle of port wine and filled a wine glass. It tasted good and warmed his insides. He took another wine glass full and felt a little tipsy. He relished the warmed-up turkey and the stuffing. He washed his plate, fork and knife, lay down on his bed and switched on the table lamp to read the afternoon paper he had bought from a kiosk round the corner. Sleep overtook him. He dozed off without switching off his table lamp.

It was a deep, dreamless slumber. He was woken by the sound of pealing church bells and realized it was time for evensong. He must have slept for over three hours. The port wine and so many hours of being by himself had given him a peculiar high and he found himself thinking of the Australian woman on the *Strathclyde* and the warmth of her hand on his thigh. He kept lying on his bed and fantasizing about Mrs Australian's bright red lips and pale breasts. But the images kept fading. His mind turned to the whore on Gerard Street who had propositioned him with the promise of giving him a good time for five pounds. What would she have done? Taken off her clothes, and his, then what? He wasn't quite sure but the possibilities gave him a painful erection. He played with himself for a while before willing himself to go no further. He used the Etonian antidote for the desire to masturbate. He went to the bathroom and poured a few jugfuls of icy cold water on the errant organ and tamed it to limpness. He decided another brisk walk in the park would clear his mind of libidinous desires.

He washed himself, made himself a cup of tea, left the radiator on to keep the flat warm and stepped out once again. The city looked even more deserted than in the morning. He did not come across a single soul from Speaker's Corner to the Serpentine. All the row boats were chained to their moorings; there were no boatmen around. A couple of old ladies were throwing crumbs of bread to ducks, geese and swans quacking and hissing around them. Otherwise the place was desolate.

Victor turned his steps homewards to his mews. At Notting Hill Gate he took Bayswater Road towards Marble Arch. There was hardly any traffic and no one on the footpaths. Near Marble Arch he came across a solitary figure clad in a flimsy raincoat, a dirty muffler wrapped round her neck. As Victor came close to her she turned round and said, 'Hello.' She was shivering in the cold.

'Hello,' replied Victor, 'what are you doing out in this cold winter evening?' She looked to be in her early twenties. Her face was bloodless white with cold.

'Waiting to earn my Christmas dinner, that's what I'm doin'. You want to give it to me? It will cost you only five pounds.'

Victor paused for a while before replying. He felt sorry for the girl, all alone in the freezing cold. 'Come. I'll give you a nice turkey dinner and Christmas pudding in my flat. It won't cost you a penny.'

The girl took a good look at Victor. He looked too young to do business with her. And though coloured, he behaved like a well-bred gentleman. She took his arm and said, 'Come along then. The name is Jenny.'

Her hands were icy cold and she continued shivering as they went along. Victor let her into his flat. 'Oo, this is nice and comfy and warm as toast.' She took off her scarf and raincoat, dumped them on the armchair and warmed herself close to the gas fire. 'Live alone 'ere?' she asked.

'Yup. When I am not at school, I have this hideout.'

'Warm and snug as a bug in a rug, ain't it? Just the place for making love.'

Victor ignored her second remark, though even as she spoke his erection had returned. 'Like a glass of mulled port wine? It will warm you.'

'That'll be nice,' she replied. 'You are a nice boy. You shouldn't be wasting your time and money on whores.'

Victor did not reply. He put the leftover turkey and Christmas pudding in the oven and turned on the radio. It was still Christmas carols. 'I love them,' said Jenny. When it came to 'Silent night, holy night', she joined in the singing.

Jenny laid the table for two, served up the turkey and the Cristmas pudding. They had more port with their dinner. Jenny washed up the dishes, forks and knives. Victor wondered whether she would leave on her own or if he would have to ask her to do so. She sensed his mood.

'You'd like to make love to me? I won't ask you for any money; you've been good to me. I'd have died of the cold.'

Victor did not answer her first question but replied, 'Don't you think you should be going home? It is very late.'

'I have nowhere to go to. Please let me stay here for the night. If you want to make love to me, I'll give you a good time. If you don't, that's fine too. But for God's sake don't throw me out. I'll die of cold lying on some footpath. Please!' She put her arms round Victor's neck and pleaded, 'Please, only for this night. I won't bother ye again, I promise,'

Victor yielded. 'Okay. You sleep on the bed; I'll sleep on the sofa.'

'O thank you!' she gushed and kissed him on his lips. 'I promise I won't bother you. I'll be gone in the morning.'

Victor got into his pajamas. He had no covering, so he decided to keep the gas fire going. Jenny stripped herself naked, tossed her clothes on top of the bed and said, 'If you feel cold, join me in the bed.'

Victor glanced at her. He would have liked to gape and stare to see what a woman's body looked like but was too polite to do so. Jenny got into the bed; Victor stretched himself on the sofa and switched off the lights. A few minutes later he could hear her snore. Sleep would not come to him. So often he had fantasized about making love to a woman, thrashing around naked in bed with her, her breasts swinging and bobbing in his face. Here he was now with a woman lying naked in his bed, more than willing to be made love to, and he was a few feet away from her, spread out on a sofa. Was he a coward? Was he an ass? Lust got the better of his doubts and fears. He got up abruptly and lay himself by the naked prostitute. 'It is cold on the sofa,' he said by way of excuse. His erect penis told another story. 'You'll be warmer in the bed, come and lie over me,' Jenny said. Victor did as she told him. She opened her legs for him. Anxious to seem in control, Victor froze above her, though his lungs threatened to explode. She did him the good turn of wrapping her legs around his waist and pulling him into her slick cunt. Victor's breath escaped him like a gale. He could not believe sex could be so thrilling— his taut body achingly alive from his head to his toes. He wished he had more arms to entwine round the girl's body and another mouth to suck both her breasts at the same time. It was his first time and lasted barely a minute. His body stiffened before he came like lava bursting out of a volcano and he yelped helplessly for longer than it had taken to spend himself. 'You finished so soon?' asked Jenny. 'Never mind; it is always like that the first time.' Half an hour later Victor was ready for more. This time Jenny put her legs on his shoulder, he plunged deeper into her with each thrust and it went on for much longer. Two hours later they were at it again. Now it was Jenny who went into a frenzy of biting, clawing and heaving, begging him to 'knock the 'ell out o' me.' So he did.

That was how Victor Jai Bhagwan lost his virginity when he was barely fourteen years old to Jenny, a flat-footed floozie of Bayswater Road. The rite of passage over, he went into the deepest slumber he had ever known.

He woke to the sound of Jenny pottering round the kitchenette making herself a cup of tea. He decided to pretend to be asleep and save himself the awkwardness of saying goodbye to her. He heard her slip on her raincoat, go down the steps, open the front door and bang it shut again. He heaved a sigh of relief and was fast asleep within seconds. He was roused by the ring of the telephone. 'Merry Christmas!' Valerie's cheerful voice came on the line. 'And how did you spend last evening?'

'Merry Christmas,' replied Victor. 'Very nice. I enjoyed the turkey and the pudding and the wine. I listened to Christmas carols. Couldn't have been nicer. Say merry Christmas on my behalf to your parents and sisters.'

Just as he returned to the sofa, the phone rang

again. 'Long distance for Mr Victor,' said the operator. 'I am Victor, please put them on.' It was his father from Delhi. 'What are you doing?' he asked.

'Enjoying myself being alone in London. How is Ma? And the girls?'

'Here, talk to them.'

He spoke to them in turns. The allotted three minutes were soon over. He went to the bathroom, had a shower and got into his clothes. He felt the hip pocket of his trousers where he kept his wallet. It was empty. He had fifteen pounds in it. He looked around the room. His Eton woollen scarf was gone. He sat down on the sofa with his head in his hands. 'The bloody bitch! She charged me her usual rate; five pounds each fuck,' he muttered. She hadn't even left him money to get back to Eton. Where would he find the bus fare?'

He spent Christmas Day in his flat reading desultorily and listening to the radio. He did not want to ruin Valerie's Christmas by telling her what had rendered him penniless. It was only the next morning on Boxing Day that he rang her up and lied. 'Valerie, my pocket was picked by someone in the crowded street. Can you lend me some money for the bus fare to school?'

She was most alarmed. 'You poor dear! You

must be more careful going into crowded places. The place is full of thieves and pickpockets. Can you manage till tomorrow? I'll be in good time to see you off in the bus for Windsor.'

'I don't need any money right now. There's everything here. Tomorrow will be fine,' he replied. He put the phone down and made a mental note not to mention anything about Jenny to the boys at Eton. If they found out he had been robbed by a whore, he would never live it down.

Valerie arrived early in the morning carrying her valise. Victor had packed his clothes and books in his haversack to return to Eton. She gave him quite a scolding before she handed him fifteen pounds. 'Never put your wallet in your hip pocket. Your father's hard-earned money gone to some street rascal. However, you've learnt a lesson. Be more careful in the future.'

She dumped her bag on the floor and went with him to see him off at the bus stand. Victor didn't have to tell her about his school scarf. She didn't ask him about it. The first thing he would do at Eton was to buy another at the school shop and no one would ask any more questions.

5

Victor's next six years were spent in Eton with vacations in Albion Mews, and short trips to Scotland, Wales, the Lake District, Stratford-on-Avon and whatever else took his fancy. He also attended debates in the House of Commons if it was discussing India and spent Sunday evenings listening to speeches at Speakers' Corner. He kept in touch with his family through weekly letters and telephone calls. In the six years he grew from the 5' 2" he was on arrival to an inch under six feet. From a pudgy little boy he became a handsome gentleman, though his voice remained a little thin, even squeaky. Years later, on the rare occasions when he was heard on All India Radio, people would remark on how much he sounded like Gandhi's other favourite Indian whose stature equalled his own.

Valerie returned to India after a six-month vacation in England. No one was quite sure why she did so as the Mattoo girls were already in college and did not need any help to get through their homework. The house ran more or less on its own with Mattoo giving orders for European meals, his wife eating her daal-roti in her room. Mattoo had provided Valerie with a single-bedroom cottage in the garden. It made life easier for them and sex more enjoyable since they could afford to be loud and furious. He saw more of her in the evenings than he did of his immediate family. Behind his back his friends described Valerie as Mattoo's Mem—white woman. Others less friendly described her as Mattoo's rakhail—mistress. Besides providing her with a home of her own in India, Mattoo assured her that the flat in Albion Mews would be hers for the rest of her life. Victor could use it whenever he was in London.

Victor finished with Eton and got admission to Balliol College, Oxford. He could have gone to any college of his choosing in Oxford or Cambridge but he chose Balliol simply because it had more Indians than any others. In the years that he had been away, his country and its people had become very precious to Victor. He wanted for them all the good things he saw in England. And he wanted to be the man who would give these to them. He happily agreed to spend the summer months before colleges opened with his family in Delhi. For his journey back home he took the Italian Lloyd Trestino boat *MV Victoria* from Genoa to Bombay. Besides an Indian prince and his family, he was the only other Indian travelling first class. He did not bother to talk to any of them nor they to him.

On the train this time from Bombay to Delhi, Victor was more alive to India than he had ever been before. The vast countryside and the seething towns seemed full of tired, dispirited people whom their gods had abandoned. They had all the world's natural resources around them and yet they were paupers beaten down by long years of colonial rule. His destiny lay among them. The British wouldn't change India, Indians themselves would. They only needed the tools of industrial growth and some initiative. That would be his mission.

At the railway station in Delhi, his father, sisters, Valerie, relatives and friends received him, all bearing garlands to put round his neck. As he stepped out of his compartment his father's staff of clerks and servants raised cries of *Jai ho! Chhote Sahib ki jai ho!*—Victory to our little master. A flower-bedecked Oldsmobile drove him home with his sisters beside him and father in the front seat. 'Where is Ma? Is she well?' asked Victor. 'She is waiting for you at home,' replied his father. 'She is in good health but didn't want to risk being in the crowd at the station.' This sounded strange to Victor and he looked at his sisters who stared back stonily and said nothing.

As the car pulled up in the portico, Victor's mother stepped over the threshold carrying a silver salver with a small mound of vermilion powder and lit with tiny silver oil lamps. She waved the salver in front of her son's face, put a mark of sindoor on his forehead, handed the salver to a servant and took her son in her embrace. 'Beta, you have taken too long to come back and see your mother.' Then she clung to him and broke down. 'Ma, what is the matter? Why are you crying? Aren't you happy to have me back?' asked Victor. She merely pulled away and looked up at him wordlessly. Then she wiped the tears off her eyes and face and rushed back to her room. 'Overcome with emotion,' pronounced his father gravely. 'She's been counting the days to your return.'

The days went by faster than Victor had anticipated. First there was his overpowering and indulgent father. He was forever inviting English judges and senior officers and rich Indian friends to show off his son. A few times he took him to the courts to hear him argue his cases. Victor was impressed that though he Lordshipped the judges, the judges were deferential towards him. He saw junior lawyers flocking to his office to prepare his briefs. Valerie—who he could see had no real reason any longer to be at Shanti Bhavan as a governess— had taken over the administration of his father's office. She made sure the clerks were on time and Mattoo's legal papers properly arranged. She joined his sisters in the evenings and read them English poetry. His sisters fussed over him, introduced their girlfriends to him and later asked him which one he liked best. There was a lot of fun and laughter. He made it a point to spend as much time as he could with his mother. In all his years he had never known her to be truly happy, but now there was something final about her sadness. When she talked to him, her apprehensions were about his health: whether he had milk every day, what he ate, making quite sure that as a Brahmin he never touched beef or alcohol. Most of all she was concerned about his marriage. 'Beta, don't ever marry a white woman; she will never fit into our family. I have been approached by top

Kashmiri families of India for their daughters, good-looking girls, highly educated. When you get back finally you must choose one you like.'

'Ma, I have no intention of marrying anyone yet. You choose a girl for me when I'm back and I will accept your choice,' he assured her every time she broached the subject. It was the least he could do for a once proud woman who had been put away like antique furniture in a corner of the sprawling house. His sisters had confirmed what he suspected—that Valerie was now effectively mistress of the house. But he could feel no ill-will or resentment towards his father or Valerie.

Before he knew it, it was time for him to take leave of his family. He had written to Gandhi asking if he could see him before returning to Oxford. Gandhi had written back on his trademark postcard telling him to come to Sabarmati any day except Tuesday which was his day of silence. So Victor took the train to Ahmedabad. This time it was only his family to see him off at the station. The next morning he reached Ahmedabad and hired a car to take him to Sabarmati ashram.

It was strange that he felt as close to Gandhi as he did to his mother, and indeed some of the things Gandhi had to say could well have come from her.

64

'I hope you have not taken to drinking; everyone in Europe drinks.'

'A little now and then, on festive occasions,' replied Victor.

'Don't touch it; it's poison.'

'Yes, Bapu. I'll do my best to avoid it.'

'You eat meat? That's also very bad. We must not kill innocent animals to fill our bellies. It is uncivilized.'

'At school they served meat at every meal. What could I do?'

'You can get good vegetarian food in London. I lived on it all the years I was there. You should abjure eating animal flesh.'

'I'll try, but I can't promise.'

'And women? The western world is full of temptations and it is easy to sin in those lands. I trust you will not succumb.'

Victor was quiet; he could not lie to Bapu. Mercifully, Bapu changed the subject.

'You still believe in industrializing India? Steel mills, textile mills and all that kind of thing? What will happen to the millions of weavers who make a living spinning and weaving cloth?'

'They could be employed in the textile mills and earn more money. We could export our cloth and earn foreign exchange.'

65

'Uproot them from their villages and put them in city slums? Not right.'

And so it went on for almost an hour till Gandhi's secretary told him he had other appointments to keep. He pulled out his pocket watch, checked the time and remarked, 'Time is sacred. Always remember that.'

'Yes, Bapu.'

He touched Gandhi's feet and took his leave. He felt exhilarated. Though he did not share Gandhi's views, in him he saw a kindred soul for whom personal destiny was no different from the destiny of his country. Even if his style turned out to be different, he knew that Gandhi's idea of sewa— service of the people—would be the guiding principle of his own life too.

From Ahmedabad Victor took the train to Bombay and from there the *MV Victoria* to Genoa. Then by train across France, across the Channel ferry to England and to his flat in Albion Mews. Valerie had hired a charwoman to come once a week to sweep the floors and dust the furniture. It was neat and tidy as it could be. To Victor this was more home than Delhi's Shanti Bhavan.

~

Victor had been to Oxford soon after he had taken his final exams in Eton. He had called on the Master of Balliol, been assured of admission and told to find his digs from the printed list the college bursar had given him. It was a short cycling distance from his college. He had filled his admission forms to study law, philosophy and economics. He had also gained admission to the Inner Temple as Gandhi has suggested. It assured him regular visits to Albion Mews after he had dined at the Temple a few evenings every session as prescribed.

At Oxford Victor came into contact with Indians of his own age. There were nearly a dozen in different colleges and they came from different parts of India. They met every fortnight at the Indian Majlis to discuss the state of affairs in their country and occasionally invited speakers from outside, conservatives, socialists and communists, to address them. Victor looked forward to these meetings and often made long interventions to air his views.

Victor tried, but could not make friends with any of the Indian boys. Three were sons of Indian princes and lived in style with cooks and servants they brought with them. They took more interest in sports and dating English girls than in studies. Victor found them too arrogant for his liking. The others were from well-to-do middle-class families or sons of senior civil servants. Their one ambition was to get into the Indian Civil Service or, failing that, to get jobs in British-owned companies in India which paid handsome salaries. They too seemed to have screwing English girls on top of their agendas; *Mem ki phuddi* was the one thing they wanted most from England, everything else was of little importance. Victor had little time for them and much preferred keeping company with the few boys he had known in Eton.

He spent his first summer vacations in Albion Mews, studying most of the day, taking long walks in Hyde Park in the afternoons. What he found a little disturbing was the sight of couples lying in tight embrace in broad daylight. Didn't they have places where they could do their love-making in privacy? He was not a prude, but the scenes lingered in his mind and disturbed his night's sleep. He tossed and turned longing for a warm body to hold.

During his vacations he paid visits to Manchester to see its latest textile mills and find out for himself why its products riled Gandhi so much. He was confirmed in his analysis that the way to drive Manchester products out of the market was to produce quality fabrics at cheaper prices in India and not return to medieval spinning and weaving. With labour cheaper than one-tenth of what it was in the western world, all India needed was the latest machines and skilled technicians. He wrote to his father and Gandhi about it. It was the same in Sheffield where he spent his days looking at steel plants. India had plenty of iron ore and coal. All it needed was modern machinery and the expertise to produce all it needed, from pen-knives and shaving blades to railway engines and bridges, and have lots to spare for export. He wrote to his father and Gandhi about this as well. Back in Oxford he propounded his views at a meeting of the Indian Majlis. They listened to him in bored silence. Victor gave up on them.

It was over a year later that Victor found an Indian he could talk to on serious subjects. He was a new entrant to Balliol and on some kind of Indian scholarship which only covered his fees and admission to an Inns of Court. He was a thin, almost gaunt, dark man with bright eyes and curly jet-black hair and a hooked nose which never stopped twitching. He reminded Victor of Shakespeare's Cassius, a man of lean and hungry look. Like Cassius in the play, this man also always seemed to be thinking too much. His name was Madhavan Nair and he was from Kerala. He was to become a person of considerable influence in Victor's life.

Nair survived on nothing else besides endless cups of tea, salted biscuits and tomato soup. Despite a tattered overcoat he wore all the time, he shivered in winter and summer. He had no small talk and was rumoured to be a communist. Victor first met him at a meeting of the Majlis at which they were discussing the role of Indian princes in the future of India. The princely types mentioned that with the experience of administering large states, some larger than provinces directly administered by the British, they had a major role to play. Nair jumped from his seat and shouted in his thick Malayali accent, 'You princes will be in garbage cans! Leeches fattened on the blood of poor peasants, you are the scum of the earth! The sooner you are wiped off the face of the of the earth, the better it will be for India.'

There was an uproar. 'Apologize!' demanded a few; others smirked. Nair stood among them, defiant and frighteningly intense. Victor was impressed by his daring. After the meeting he went up to Nair and shook his claw-like hand. 'I am Jai Bhagwan from Delhi. I agree with everything you said.' They became friends.

Nair was not a card-carrying member of the Communist Party but of the Indian National Congress (Gandhi) and joined the Labour Party's left-wing Socialist group in London. He had come from India with introductions from his sponsors and with some English radicals formed The Free India Society. It had no more than two dozen members to start with, mostly men and women who came from the upper echelons of English society. They welcomed Nair in their homes; he was exotic enough and gave them the chance to be seen as radical and fashionably leftist. A couple of English girls were very taken up by his austere appearance and wanted to mother him. He had no trouble in taking them to bed. He was short and peremptory with them afterwards, but they usually came right back.

Nair was utterly unlike Victor but they hit it off from the very start. Victor liked his sharp wit and ability to give more tit for tat he got from adversaries in debates. He also had a phenomenal memory and could reel out statistics to prove how the British had milked India over the centuries. Nair, on the other hand, was pleased with Victor's high opinion of him and saw himself as a sort of intellectual mentor of the rich young Indian. Though Victor was not much into politics, he joined Nair's Free India Society.

They spent most of their after-college hours together. Victor often invited him out for dinner. He was a poor eater; it was invariably tomato soup and

71

toast accompanied by relays of cups of tea. He would not eat meat nor take beer or wine. 'You are a bit of an ascetic, you know,' said Victor to him one evening. 'How you manage to survive in this damp, cold climate is beyond me.'

Nair grinned. 'The body does not need all the junk you people dump into it morning, noon and night. It all comes out as smelly shit.' They talked endlessly; Nair about the need to throw the British out of India; Victor about how India could be made rich and prosperous.

'Look, why don't you put your ideas on paper? I'll help you. Let other people know about your dreams for India,' said Nair another evening.

'Me, write? Don't be ridiculous,' said Victor. 'I couldn't write even if my life depended on it. I only write letters to my parents. I haven't even written a love letter.'

'You can always start. Write a long love letter of many chapters to India as if it were your sweetheart.'

'Who will read my junk? It will be a waste of time. Besides, I have to prepare for my exams; Oxford and Bar finals. Where is the time?'

'Find it. Instead of yakking away evening after evening, write a page a day and get it out of your system.'

72

'Who'll publish it?'

'Leave that to me. You write the book, I'll get it published. We have Free India publications.'

The idea germinated in Victor's mind. How wonderful it would be to have a book with his name printed on the cover. See it displayed in windows of bookstores across the globe. Have people coming to ask him to autograph copies for them. It was like a fever. It was the inception of *India of My Dreams* by Victor Jai Bhagwan.

Victor studied hard for his exams and at the same time kept making notes for his book. He discussed every chapter with Nair before preparing a draft; then showed him his final version. As soon as his exams were over, he got down to his book. One month in Albion Mews and the book was done. He handed over the manuscript to Nair when he was in London to dine at his Inns of Court. A month later he received a contract from Left Book Publishers. Victor was in seventh heaven and sent a long telegram to his father. He got a congratulatory telegram in return and his first buyer: he was to ship 500 copies to his father for free distribution to his friends and mail one autographed copy to Gandhi at Sabarmati.

Victor hoped to get a first division; he got only a second. He was not unduly upset. His degree from

Oxford saved him from taking Bar exams. He got his Barrister's certificate. He had visiting cards printed: V. Jai Bhagwan BA (Oxon) Barrister-at-Law. A couple of hundred cards had his Albion Mews address; another 200 his father's.

Despite his father's suggestion that he see more of Europe before returning home, Victor decided to stay on in London. The city had grown on him. He loved loitering around Central London, watching people feed pigeons in Trafalgar Square, listening to the twittering of thousands of starlings at dusk, gazing at shop windows and crowds hurrying by. And of course there was Hyde Park with its Speakers' Corner, street walkers along Bayswater Road and above all the snug peacefulness of his tiny apartment. He did, however, spend another few days in Manchester. He called on the general manager of the largest textile mill in England and asked him if he would be interested in a partnership to set up a modern textile mill in India. 'I'll have to consult my board of directors,' the manager replied cagily. 'We have our hands full; I am not sure how they will respond to the idea. I will let you know in three days.' As Victor had anticipated, the response was negative. Why should they break their legs with their own hands by encouraging and abetting Indian products? Victor was undaunted. He approached manufacturers of textile machinery; they were more than happy to sell the latest machines at reasonable prices. He approached architects who had designed the mills and technicians who had installed the machines. A three-month assignment in India with handsome wages was more than they could resist. Victor took down their names and addresses and promised to send them formal contracts as soon as he was ready to send for them. In an almost matter-of-fact manner, he had set in motion the momentous project that would shape his own future and India's.

6

Victor left some of his clothes and other belongings in his London flat, so that Valerie understood it was his for whenever he wanted it, and headed back home to Delhi. He reached Shanti Bhavan loaded with gifts for everyone: a gold fountain pen for his father, a mohair shawl for his mother, scarves and bottles of perfumes for his sisters, an illustrated Bible for Valerie. As he had hoped, many of his father's friends came to have his book autographed by him. He did not ask them if they had read it.

After the returning home celebrations and excitement was over, his father asked him at the breakfast table, 'So Jai, what now?'

Without a pause he replied, 'I want to set up the

biggest and the most modern textile factory in India, either here or in Bombay or Ahmedabad. I will have to raise the money to buy land and import machinery from England. I have brought the details of what I will need with me.'

Mattoo thought this over the problem before he replied. 'I don't have that kind of money saved up. We will have to float a public company and invite people to buy shares. I am sure some of my rich clients will pitch in. But we must keep the control in our own hands. You look for the proper site; it will be easier to get one near Delhi than any other city. I'll get land agents to take you around to see what is available.'

There were days of hectic activity. Victor was out most of the day. He needed a minimum of fifteen acres with immediate possession of undisputed land. It was the mid 1930s and prime land was already becoming scarce. At last he found one stretch adjacent to a village some ten miles upstream of the Yamuna. It was barren because of saltpetre. He called a panchayat of the village and asked them if they objected to having a mill go up next to their village. He knew that if he wanted the project to be a success, he had to take them with him. 'I will give you whatever you think a reasonable price for the barren piece of land. I will also give your boys and girls employment.'

They were overjoyed. 'Give us what you think is reasonable. Your coming will bring light to our village. Our generations to come will bless you.'

'Grow cotton, good quality cotton,' he told them, 'I will buy whatever you grow.'

He joined them smoking the hookah of goodwill that went from mouth to mouth. Old women came up and put their hands on his head to bless him; young women peered through their half-drawn veils; boys and girls just stood around gaping and giggling. Victor was a happy man that day: the first hurdle had been crossed.

He broke the good news to his family. His father had meanwhile drawn up the articles of association of the new company. He would be chairman for life; Victor its general manager. His mother and sisters would be allotted shares. The rest was to be thrown open to the public. The company would be known as Jai Bhagwan Textiles.

The next day Victor took an architect with him and got the tehsildar to join them. They put markers at different places. Victor told the architect that he was only to design workers' quarters: three rooms with a small courtyard, latrine and washroom. The rest would be designed by an architect he was getting from England. He wrote to Nair inviting him to be the company's agent in England, offering him a handsome salary, travelling expenses, perks and commission on sales. He was to finalize negotiations with the architect and mechanics in Manchester. Nair was thrilled. He had never seen so much money; he could live comfortably in London after he had finished with Oxford. The prospects of his making a living in legal practice were bleak. He accepted Victor's offer with alacrity.

Victor was like a man possessed. Even before the English architect, technicians and crates of spinning and weaving machinery were ploughing the seas on cargo boats, he was planning to replicate the model to be set up near different cities of the country and offering jobs at higher salaries to cotton mill workers employed in existing mills.

A month later the architect arrived carrying designs of mills he had set up in Manchester. Two months later came the machines. Because he knew it would make her happy, Victor got his mother to perform bhoomi pooja and lay the foundation stone. Jai Bhagwan Textiles began to take concrete shape. Six months later the mill was ready to go. Mattoo invited the Viceroy to the inauguration function: he could not very well ask Mahatma Gandhi to come to the function. It was attended by the elite of the city including cloth merchants big and small. The Viceroy pressed the button to get the machines going. Guests were taken around the mill to see how different varieties of textiles were made. They were served tea, sandwiches and cakes. As they left, they were given parcels containing products of the mill as presents: bed sheets, table cloths, sarees, curtains, furnishing fabrics, towels and napkins. No other textile mill in India was producing as many different items at the same time. Victor had no belief in small beginnings; Jai Bhagwan Textiles would be the biggest mill in the country.

Victor sent a parcel of his products to the Mahatma in Sabarmati Ashram with a letter asking for his blessings and telling him to dispose of the items as he thought fit. A few days later he received a postcard with a cryptic two-word acknowledgement: *Jeetey raho*—long may you live.

Money started rolling in. After paying dividends to shareholders, Victor ploughed profits into setting up more textile mills: one in every state of India. Many old mills went into liquidation. He bought them and renovated them. 'Modernize or perish' was the motto he gave to Indian industrialists. Within two years there were not enough British textiles for the Mahatma and his followers to make bonfires of; Indian fabrics had taken over the Indian market and were being exported to some foreign countries too.

Even as his first few textile mills were being set up, Victor decided on sugar mills as well. The English made sugar out of beetroot; he imported machinery from other countries which made it out of sugar cane. Another chain of mills, Jai Bhagwan Sugar Mills, came up in cane-producing states.

Victor and his vision of progress were taking India by storm. In barely five years he had set up mills in a fourth of the country. Little townships were beginning to grow around his large factories. He paid his workers unheard of salaries, built housing colonies for them, and made sure all his products were priced low. Money was good, but that was not why he had set up his mills; his true ambition was to make prosperity possible for every Indian. One of his sisters said to him one day that he was working too hard and aiming too high—he was barely thirty, after all. He replied: 'I am a volcano; there is so much energy in me because there is so much to be done in this country. I cannot take it easy.'

Over the next couple of years Victor set up factories to produce chemicals, cement and bicycles, before finally investing significant capital in shipping. This last made it necessary for him to move much of his business operations to Bombay. He bought a few nondescript blocks of apartments on Marine Drive and built a thirty-storeyed building, Jai Bhagwan Towers. It was the first of its kind in India. He kept the penthouse and the floor below for his residence, the rest for different departments of the industrial empire he had created.

Through all this, Victor kept aloof from the ferment of the freedom struggle. He was no supporter of the Raj, but he had no flair for politics. Men like Nair understood politics better, they could outshine and out-shout the ideologues of colonialism. Besides, there were Bapu Gandhi and his followers working to throw the British out. To Victor it was more important to industralize India, to make it economically strong. Because what freedom could there be without that? There was so much the country needed to modernize itself: produce more electricity to bring light in every home and drive machines; lay highways and rail lines to connect remote villages to cities and towns; manufacture chemical fertilizers and pesticides to boost agricultural production; and even manufacture its own automobiles, ships and aircraft. The scope was endless.

It was for the government to take the initiative. Even if the British thought it worth their while to do so, they were now so engrossed in a life-and-death struggle against fascist powers that to think of anything besides winning the war was looked upon as treason. They had committed themselves to hand over power to the Indians as soon as the war was over. Few Indians, including Gandhi, trusted them to keep their word. Victor did. And he didn't want a free india to start off as a backward, impoverished nation.

All his many enterprises had made record profits during the war. Congress leaders contacted him once in a while through Gandhi for funds and he always obliged, but discreetly. He had been approached by the Viceroy to join his council but he had turned down the offer with a polite refusal. He could not be a member of a government which put Bapu Gandhi and other national leaders in jail. He preferred to bide his time, and if the rulers of independent India wanted his advice and counsel in any capacity, he would consider their invitation favourably.

7

The hectic pace of work in which Victor involved all members of his family save his mother left little time for them to settle personal affairs. Mattoo was earning more as president of Victor's many companies than he had as a lawyer. (He would still not let go of Valerie Bottomley as his personal secretary; she showed no inclination to return to England.) They had become India's richest family; but to Victor's mother this meant little. 'You've all got caught in the web of Maya,' she said to them one day when Valerie was not around. 'Have you ever thought about the marriage of your three sisters, Jai Bhagwan? Or yours?' Her husband replied, 'I have been approached by many well-to-do families including those of rulers of states but I put them off. On one thing I am quite certain: I will not give any of my daughters to the son of a raja. I know many of them; they are drunkards and debauches, they have no family life. I told them we are Brahmins, you are Rajputs; there can't be matrimonial alliances between us. It is forbidden by our dharma.' They had a hearty laugh. All except his wife, who had her views on Mattoo's own integrity as a family man. 'What about others?' she asked impatiently. 'Haven't you found anyone good enough for my daughters?'

'They can have the pick of this country,' replied Mattoo. 'I'll have the boys come over in turns and leave the choice to the girls.'

So it came to be. Every one of the Mattoo girls, though well over the marriageable age by Indian standards, was worth a tidy fortune: besides chests full of jewellery and priceless saris there were agencies of Jai Bhagwan companies going with them. The eldest girl picked a boy in the Indian Civil Service who had done a year's probation in Oxford. He was a Bengali. The second picked a boxwala recruited by Burma Shell soon after he had taken his degree from Cambridge. He was a Punjabi. The third chose the son of a Gujarati textile manufacturer of Ahmedabad who had managed to keep afloat by modernizing his mill. None of them was a Brahmin. When it came to their marriages, Victor put his foot down. 'We must set an example to our countrymen. There must be no lavish display of wealth, no big baraats or bands, exploding of fireworks and that kind of vulgarity. We will make it clear that only immediate members of the grooms' families are welcome in our home— a simple Hindu wedding ceremony. One dinner party. And they depart.'

There were no dissenting voices. So in one year the three Mattoo girls got married without many people getting to know. Only Victor was still to find a wife.

'What about you, beta?' his mother asked after her daughters had left. 'Won't I have a grandson of my own?'

'Ma, I have told you many times. I will marry any girl who you think will make a good daughter-in-law for you.' Love had given Victor the miss. He hadn't the time or even the need any more for romance and passion. He had promised his mother he would marry the girl of her choice. There was no reason not to fulfil her wish.

'I have one in mind,' said his mother excitedly. 'She is the daughter of a distant cousin, a Raina. A very humble ghareloo girl. I don't know if she will fit into your English ways, all the kaanta-chhuri (fork and knife) style. She is only a matriculate and doesn't speak much English. But like all Kashmiri girls she is fair. What I like most about her is her humility. If you approve of her I will be happy. If you do not, I will look for another Kashmiri girl.'

'Ma, if she is the one you like best, I will be happy to make you happy. What is her name?'

'Jaishree. Jaishree Raina. She's been here with her mother a few times but you never bothered to look at them.'

As a matter of fact Victor had seen this girl with her mother a couple of times when they were being escorted by his mother's maidservant to her room. She looked like a callow little schoolgirl, somewhat overawed by the size of the house, like many visitors were. 'Ma, you talk to Papa; if he is agreeable you can ask the girl's mother on my behalf.'

That evening Victor's mother broached the subject with her husband, half expecting to be snubbed by him. She was pleasantly surprised by his reaction. 'At least one of our children will be married to a Kashmiri Pandit and our line will not be dissolved into the rest of India,' he said. 'They are a very maamooli (ordinary) family; not our class. I think her father is a small-time commission agent living in a gali where many poor Kashmiri Pandit families live. But money is of no consequence; we can give him an outlet or two for our products to improve his financial status. If your beta agrees, I have no objection.'

Mattoo had a guilty conscience about the way he had put aside his wife in a corner of the house and made Valerie Bottomley his concubine. So often, even as he ground into Valerie, like the savage that she begged him to be with her, he was aware of his wife sobbing in her room. Because he had wanted it so, all other members of the family had taken to speaking English which she did not understand. They ate western food which she did not. He had condemned her to a life of silence and loneliness. He wanted to make amends by giving her a companion of her choice.

Victor's thoughts were along the same lines. He was not anxious to take a wife. He had shied away from entering into emotional relationships with the few English girls he had met in college. No sooner had one got close to him than she wanted to invade his private space and assert exclusive proprietary rights over him. He was reluctant to have sex with any of them because he sensed that sexual relationship was a kind of temporary marriage which conferred emotional rights on both partners. He much preferred consorting with prostitutes whenever he could. He got the sex he wanted; she got the money she wanted. No hassles, no emotional baggage. It also occurred to him that he had never had sex with an Indian woman. Nor with a virgin. Would it be any different than with the whores he had picked up on the streets round Piccadilly Circus or Bayswater Road? There was every chance, in fact, that Jaishree Raina might turn out to be just the sort of wife he wanted. There was little likelihood of her claiming equality with him. She would be like his mother who bore her husband children and returned to the part of the house allotted to her.

Victor's marriage was as low-key as those of his sisters. No invitation cards were printed. Only his sisters and their husbands came to Delhi for the occasion. The wedding rites took place in Shanti Bhavan. Jaishree's parents left after the ceremony was over, leaving their youngest child to the care of the Mattoo family.

Victor took Jaishree on the night of their marriage. She was barely seventeen and a virgin. She bled profusely but bore the pain without complaining. No words of love were exchanged between them. In fact, few words were exchanged between them at all.

Victor took her every night and sometimes during the afternoon siesta. It was the only bond they shared. And since neither one expected more from the marriage than this simple contract of duty and sex, they were content. Victor divided his time between Shanti Bhavan in Delhi and Jai Bhagwan Towers in Bombay. Jaishree never left Delhi and spent much of her time in her mother-in-law's room, except when Victor was in town. Less than two months after their marriage, Jaishree missed her first period. And then the second. When the third period was due she began to throw up in the mornings. Victor's mother was delighted. She wrote to her daughters giving them the good news. She would soon have a grandson in her lap and they a nephew to play with when they came to Delhi. Mattoo began planning his grandson's education. Victor, though a little bemused, was happy enough at the prospect of having an heir.

The joy was short-lived. Jaishree died giving birth to her child, a daughter. It was the first death in the large house which was now enveloped in gloom. Victor was numbed with anguish. He had not said a loving word to his wife of ten months. Whenever he was in Shanti Bhavan, he had expected to find her in their bedroom, waiting for him to come in, shut the door, undress and mount her. Some days the sight of her slender naked body startled him. She was a mere child! Where had she learned to handle the fevered needs of a man almost twice her age? He felt a tenderness towards his submissive girl-wife. He had wanted to tell her this one day and do better by her than his father had done by his mother. Now it was too late. His normally in-control father took the tragedy very badly and lost his zest for life. Even Valerie was unable to console him. Surprisingly enough, the one who took it in her stride as the will of an inscrutable God was Victor's mother. Though the child was not the grandson that she wanted but a granddaughter, she ascribed that too to God's will and was content to abide with it. Now she would be a grandmother as well as a mother to the newborn babe. She arranged for a wet nurse with a one-month old baby to move into Shanti Bhavan to suckle her granddaughter.

Mattoo chose the name for the newborn—Bharati. Victor's mother would not let Bharati out of her sight. She watched her being breastfed by the wet nurse, put her on her shoulder to let her burp, bathed her, changed her clothes and lay beside her in bed. Often Bharati's podgy hands went searching for her bosom and she would sigh and say, 'Beti, there is nothing left there for you; Ayah, she is hungry, give her another feed.'

Mattoo was also taken up by his granddaughter and spent hours talking to the baby and begging her to give him a smile. Valerie would join the others in baby worship. 'Pretty, isn't she? Taken after her father: his features, her mother's complexion. She'll grow up into a stunning beauty, God willing.'

The first three words Bharati learnt to babble were Dadima, Dadoo, and Gannyma, to refer to Victor's mother, Mattoo and Valerie. Papi, for her father, was the fourth; he spent less time with her than the others.

~

Victor shuttled between Delhi and Bombay more frequently now and worked almost sixteen hours a day. He had no choice. Mattoo, approaching seventy and badly affected by Jaishree's death, was growing indifferent to office work, and Victor had to take on more on his shoulders. His shipping business was also not doing as well as he had hoped. He had appointed his good friend Nair general manager of Jai Bhagwan Shipping Company after the latter returned from London, fleeing an enraged British

Parliamentarian he had insulted in public. With the cushy job, Victor also provided Nair a large flat in Jai Bhagwan Towers and other benefits like a chauffeur-driven car, the right to spend as much on entertainment as he thought proper, the right to hire and fire his staff as he pleased. But Nair was not pulling his weight. He had a prickly personality and did not get on well with any of his senior executives. It was said that he had given a senior position to his mistress who had once worked in the typing pool. He was also reported to be taking commissions on tramp ships he bought for the company. In the business circles of Bombay he had the reputation of being rude and arrogant. Some complaints Victor received were from senior staff who resigned their jobs; many more of Nair's peccadilloes came in anonymous letters. Victor took no notice of them. He had implicit trust in Nair's integrity and refused to hear anything said against him; he even ignored his father's advice to send Nair back to England because he was giving the company a bad name in India.

Whenever Victor was in Bombay, Nair fawned over him: his flattery was subtle and hence more acceptable to Victor than the blatant praises others showered on him. It did not occur to him to wonder at the change in Nair's attitude towards him. When they were students in London, Nair had made no secret of the fact that he considered himself intellectually superior to Victor. He took obvious satisfaction in guiding Victor and lecturing him on communism. He was never rude or sharp with Victor but did tick him off once in a while for his 'bourgeois' ways; he himself was a communist who starved himself and wore a tattered coat, which again made him feel superior. This did not bother Victor who liked having as a friend the witty, normally acerbic younger man who was a star in the liberal circles of London. Now, it was Nair who referred to Victor as the star. He agreed with everything Victor said and rarely voiced his own opinion on any matter. Had Victor been observant, he would have noticed that Nair's fists clenched whenever he spoke to Victor and he rarely looked him in the eye. The truth was that Victor's great success had changed the equation between them and this had made Nair bitter. He resented the fact that Victor was his mentor now. He resented it more because he needed this patronage. Victor was oblivious to this. Whenever people said anything against Nair, he either snubbed them or replied with a stony silence. He worked harder to cover up for Nair's inefficiency; he was not one to admit failure in any business he undertook. But this meant that he had to spend much more time in Bombay than in Delhi.

Victor could not come to terms with Bombay's upper-class society. Most of them had businesses of different kinds with single-track minds: how to make more money and cheat their workers and the income tax authorities. Their transactions were largely in unaccounted cash. The future of their country was of little concern to them. They lived in opulent splendour without any refinement. Victor kept aloof from them, but the rest of the city's inhabitants weren't his kind of people either—there was too big a divide of class and temperament between him and the masses. He had to spend many days of the month in Bombay but wanted to have as little to do with its citizens as possible. He also wanted to be away from his office where people complained constantly about Nair. He found the ideal solution. Once when abroad looking for ships to add to his fleet, he heard about a yacht owned by a Greek millionaire who had died recently which was on sale. He flew to Athens to see it. It was a motorized vessel without sails. It had twelve cabins, a large lounge and a dining room. He closed the deal and ordered the captain to deliver it at Bombay where his Indian crew would take over.

Victor returned home. He looked as if he had found a new wife for himself. He showed pictures of his new toy to his family and told them how many people it could accommodate, how fast it could travel—from Karachi to Bombay to Goa to Madras to Calcutta, all in one week! 'What will you do with it?' asked his mother naively. 'Do with it, Ma? I will live in it, conduct my business, have board meetings, have parties. Wait till you see it. You will fall in love with it—no noise, no khich pich, no smells. Only fresh air and the boundless sea. I want all of you to come to Bombay and see it.'

When he got news of the arrival of the yacht, he chartered a Dakota to fly his entire family to Bombay. They spent a night in the penthouse of Jai Bhagwan Towers. Next morning they were driven up to the Yacht Club close to the Gateway of India where the yacht was moored. A crowd had collected there; no one had seen a yacht of that size and elegance. Victor's mother had already chosen a name for it: *Jal Bharati*.

The family were shown around the yacht. They saw their names on doors of cabins meant for them. They stood on the deck and waved to the crowds. With the hoot of a siren that echoed across Marine Drive the *Jal Bharati* pulled away from the Yacht

Club of India and headed towards Elephanta. It was a family picnic. They visited the caves and returned to the yacht for lunch. Everyone was very excited, most of all Bharati, now four years old. She went around telling everyone, pointing to the yacht, 'My sip.'

'Yes, beta,' assured her Dadima, 'your Papi has got it for you.'

They sailed to Goa and spent two days on shore walking on its sea beaches.

'Could do with a few good hotels,' remarked Victor. 'This place could draw tourists from all the world. But only after we've got rid of the Portuguese. They have no business to be here. Now that the war is over, it is only a matter of time before the British leave India. Once we get them out we will send the French and the Portuguese packing.'

Victor wrote to Gandhi about his new acquisition. As usual he got a prompt reply on a postcard. It contained a mild snub: 'Always keep your poor countrymen in mind. Don't let your new acquisition become a rich man's toy.'

Victor was provoked to defend himself. He wrote back: 'Bapu, however different our perceptions about the future of our country may be, you have been the source of my inspiration. You have the right to rebuke me about what you describe as my expensive toy. But I do not mean to play with it; I mean to conduct my business on its board far away from the maddening crowd. You know I have done my little bit for my countrymen. I have given employment to over 100,000 men and women. I give them free housing and their children free education and medical care. I give them retirement benefits and provident funds. Surely you approve of these things. I would be happy to hear you say so if you do.'

Bapu relented, once again with a cryptic one-liner: 'I look upon you as my own son, I don't have to say more.'

8

The family and servants were flown back to Delhi after a few weeks. Victor stayed back in Bombay. There were a few changes in his daily routine. At first he spent the night and most of the day in his penthouse and offices in Jai Bhagwan Towers and took *Jal Bharati* 'for a spin', as he said, for a couple of hours in the evening. Then he reversed his daily schedule; he spent his nights on the yacht, spent a few hours in his office and returned to the boat in the afternoon. And he rediscovered the peace he had known all those years ago when he spent time alone at his flat in Albion Mews. He felt confident about handling anything when he was by himself on his yacht. He began to value the solitude, which he could not explain to his ageing parents. They often suggested that he marry again. He brushed aside the idea each time. He was not looking for a companion: he had no time for companionship. Though at times he longed for physical intimacy with a young woman, whenever one made overtures to him, he did not respond to her. He did not want a mistress either, because having one would impose certain emotional obligations. And give rise to gossip. So would consorting with an Indian prostitute. Whoring in London, Paris and Hamburg was wiser than whoring in Bombay or Delhi. In any case his mind was preoccupied with things more important than sex.

The British had finally decided to hand India over to Indians. But the country was to be split in two. Fratricidal war erupted on the subcontinent between Hindus and Sikhs on the one side and Muslims on the other. They were slitting each other's throats from the banks of the Indus to beyond the Hooghly. This was not the India Victor had dreamt of in his younger days. He was in Delhi the day India gained her independence. The city was flooded with Hindu and Sikh refugees who had fled from Pakistan. They were driving Muslims out of their homes and shops. They were living in ancient monuments, on footpaths and roundabouts. His father had employed extra guards and shut the gates of his house to prevent them occupying his garden. He was in a high state of tension, blabbering nonsense: 'Keep the British here, we are not fit to rule this country . . . all this talk of freedom is *buk buk* . . . we are born to be slaves.' It was no use talking to him. And Bapu Gandhi had vanished into remote villages of East Bengal, to tell people to behave like civilized human beings because they were all children of the same God known by different names. The only one who looked happy was Victor's little daughter, who went around Shanti Bhavan marching like a soldier carrying the tricoloured flag of Independent India and shouting '*Bharat Mata ki Jai* (Long live Mother India)!; *Mahatma Gandhi ki Jai*; *Inquilab zindabad* (Long live the revolution)!'

Victor did not take part in any of the Independence Day celebrations in Delhi and returned to Bombay. The city was also in a festive mood with the Indian flag flying on all buildings and processions marching down the streets shouting slogans. Nair had himself hoisted the tricolour on Jai Bhagwan Towers and treated the entire staff to tea and cheap biscuits. He was jubilant: he had been elected president of the state Bombay committee and assured of a seat in Parliament. Victor spent an hour in his penthouse and without informing anyone drove to the Gateway of India to board his yacht. He told the captain to take the boat out into the open sea till land was out of sight and weigh anchor there. He wanted to be by himself, undisturbed.

He felt more isolated than ever before. The country he thought was his, for whose prosperous future he had been laying strong foundations, had been transformed into something completely unrecognizable by the British, the Congress and the Muslim League. Politics had won after all. In his personal life too things were changing for the worst. His father's health was deteriorating. The babbling with which he had responded to Independence and the Partition refugees had forced everyone to confront the obvious: he was very ill. He had become absent-minded and had bouts of depression followed by hyperactivity during which he talked non-stop by the hour. His only companion was the doughty Valerie Bottomley who did her best to keep his office going, get doctors, give him medicines on time and try to cheer him up. Victor's mother seemed to enjoy her husband's growing helplessness. If he could show such callous indifference to her for all these years of her married life he had no right to expect her to look after him when he was stricken. Her sole interest in life seemed to be her granddaughter Bharati. Victor sensed that his father's days were numbered. But for his father's support he would not have got where he had. He now had to reconcile himself to the idea of not having him around for too long.

There was a time when he had hoped for support from another man: his old friend Nair. But he had changed. Victor had turned a deaf ear to all that was being said about him. He still refused to take any such talk seriously. But he could see that Nair harboured other ambitions than being his number two and overall general manager of his companies. He persuaded Victor to give large donations to the Congress Party and entertained editors of left-wing journals. It was evident that he wanted to build a career in politics with the support of Jai Bhagwan Enterprises. It made Victor uneasy. He would not stand in Nair's way but he could no longer count on him to forward his future plans. For the first time in his life, Victor understood the meaning of loneliness.

~

It did not take long for Victor's gloomy prophecies to come true. It was a sunny October morning. Victor was taking in the sea air on a deck chair when he saw a motor boat come streaming across the bay and pull up alongside *Jal Bharati*. 'An urgent telegram for the sahib,' yelled the pilot of the boat. It was a short message from Valerie: 'Your father suffered a stroke and haemorrhage of the brain. Condition serious. Come at once. Have informed your sisters.'

Victor ordered the yacht back to the harbour. His car was waiting for him. He asked his secretary to hire a private aircraft from the Tatas. Nair had decided to accompany him. Late that afternoon, as they stepped down the tarmac at Delhi's Palam Airport and proceeded towards the airport building, they were accosted by a party of press photographers and reporters. Victor sensed that the event he dreaded had taken place. He brushed the journalists aside and walked ramrod straight through the arrivals lounge to the car awaiting him where there was another group of reporters. Nair spoke sharply to the pressmen. 'Have you no shame? He's just heard of his father's death and you want to interview him! This is ghoulish. Move away!' Then he took Victor by the arm and led him into the car. The old Nair had surfaced briefly, and Victor felt both affection and gratitude; he couldn't have wished for anyone else to be by his side at this difficult time.

Press cars followed his right to his home. The road outside and the lawns were full of mourners.

Liveried chaprasis were bringing in wreaths to be placed on Mattoo's body, from the Governor General, Prime Minister, cabinet ministers, heads of industrial houses. No sooner had they heard that Victor had arrived than they would come to pay their condolences—and be photographed doing so. Grief which was private to him and his family would be converted into an exercise in public relations. Valerie Bottomley stepped out of the crowd and embraced Victor. 'You are a source of strength to everyone; I'll leave you with your mother and daughter.' She slipped out of the crowd and returned to her cottage. She knew she was not wanted anymore.

Victor took off his shoes and entered the drawing room where his father's body had been laid on the floor amidst large blocks of ice. Incense of agarbatti mingled with the scent of dying flowers. Priests seated in a corner chanted Sanskrit shlokas that few people understood, but the drone was preferable to silence. His mother sat by her husband's head, moaning and breaking into sobs. Bharati sat next to her, weeping silently. Mattoo lay with his mouth half open and cotton swabs stuck in his nostrils. Victor sat down on the floor and took his mother and daughter in his arms. His resolve broke down and he wept like a child. Bharati looked up at him and stopped crying. She stared at him in shock. 'Don't cry Papi,' she implored. 'You scare me, Papi.' Victor hugged her tight and promised, 'I won't, my child. We must all be strong. I want you to be strong too, for your Dadima.' Both father and daughter wiped their tears. Even as they composed themselves the Governor General arrived to condole with Victor. While they met and spoke in hushed, sad tones, seven-year-old Bharati took charge. She ordered the durbaan not to allow anyone into the room without first checking with sahib. 'My father is very tired. We must look after him,' she said firmly to the astonished durbaan who clicked his heels, saluted the little lady and said, 'Ji Memsahib!'

After the mourners had left, Victor went to Valerie's cottage. Though just a short walk from the main house, it looked forlorn with its single lit window in the night. It seemed she had been expecting him. 'Come Victor, you could do with a stiff drink or two. I've also got some chicken sandwiches to share with you. I know there'll be no food cooked in the house today.' She poured out two large Scotch and sodas and handed him a glass. Victor could see that she had been crying. And he noticed for the first time that she was now an old woman.

'He had a good innings,' said Valerie breaking

the ice. 'And he did his family and friends well. He was very good to me.' She brushed a tear from the corner of one eye.

'He was a good father,' responded Victor. 'I have much to be grateful for to him.'

They sat in silence for some time. Then Valerie spoke. 'I expect I won't be needed around here anymore. I think I should return to England. My parents are in their nineties and I am not getting any younger. But we'll keep in touch, won't we?'

'Of course!' replied Victor. 'You've been like a member of the family. You have the use of the Albion Mews flat whenever you are in London. You have a handsome provident fund. And I will always be there if you need anything.'

'Bless you, Victor. I am well provided for by God's grace, your father and you. Don't worry about me. Go and join your family. Your sisters should have arrived by now.'

As he left, Victor said, 'Thank you, Valerie. I know you brought happiness into my father's life. I want you to know I'm grateful to you for that.'

Valerie's eyes welled up. She felt a huge weight had been lifted off her heart. 'Thank you, Victor. God be with you always.'

His sisters and their husbands arrived for the

funeral the next morning. Preparations for the funeral began early. Mattoo's body was bathed in water specially brought overnight from Haridwar. It was draped in white from head to foot, laid on two planks of wood and tied to them by a rope. The hearse drove in at 8.45 a.m.

Victor watched his mother touch her unfaithful husband's feet. The body was lifted into the hearse. She wept like a child as the hearse drove away. As it left the outer gate of the house, over fifty cars followed it on its journey to the river. There were policemen posted all along the route to halt traffic till the cortege had passed.

There was an enormous crowd on the Yamuna's bank: ministers of government mingled with workers from Jai Bhagwan Textiles. Hundreds of wreaths were laid on the pyre and then removed. At 11 a.m. Victor was handed a flaming torch. He went round the pyre, setting it aflame at different points. It burst into flames, the crackling of wood drowned by the drone of shlokas chanted by a choir of a dozen Brahmin priests. Victor felt a wave of panic rise in the pit of his stomach at the absolute finality of this parting. He waited for it to pass. Bharati came up to him and put her small hand in his. Then he was calm.

A postcard from Bapu Gandhi arrived that evening: 'Death is an integral part of life. It comes to all of us in due course of time. Do not grieve too much. Just meditate on what your father left you in his legacy and build on it. You will emerge from this stronger. In your hour of bereavement I send you, your dear mother and daughter and all other members of your family my love. Yours, Bapu.' Victor put the card in his pocket; it would be his most cherished possession.

A week later, Valerie Bottomley took leave of the Mattoo family. Victor and Bharati drove her to Palam Airport for the long flight to London. She would never see India again.

Victor's brother-in-law who was in the ICS and posted in Delhi was persuaded to move into the house with his wife and their children to give company to and look after Victor's mother and daughter. Victor returned to Bombay. For close to three months after he had consigned his father to the flames and then his ashes to the Ganga, he was at a loose end. He had a sense that tragedy was not done with him yet. The feeling frustrated him—it kept him from giving one hundred per cent to his work. He decided to take a break and went on a long cruise in his yacht. He was anchored near Goa when the news reached him. He had lost his second father: Bapu had been assassinated. He was devastated. What kind of savage race did he belong to which killed its own saintly father? He did not know who to turn to for solace. He felt being on a luxury yacht off the coast of Goa was not the right place to be at the time. He returned to Bombay and after a day attending a condolence meeting called by his staff, flew to Delhi to be with his mother. She was in a state of shock. She held her frail head in her hands and kept repeating, 'It is kalyug (the dark age). People are killing their own fathers! Who knows when they will come for us. Look after yourself, beta. These are bad times.'

'Don't worry about me, Ma. No one is going to kill me,' he assured her. 'I haven't done enough good to people yet.'

He drove to the cremation site at Nigambodh Ghat that night. He sat there till morning, watching the dying embers in the funeral pyres. He meant to look death in the face. As dawn broke, he wasn't sure if he had, but he felt less diminished. He would go back and continue his efforts for India's prosperity, whether India deserved it or not.

9

Years passed. Victor immersed himself in his work, spending more time in Jai Bhagwan Towers than he would have wished and travelling to his mills and factories all over the country. His shipping business remained a worry, but with Nair's political activities taking up much of his time, Victor could bring in new, efficient managers without causing Nair any unhappiness.

If you took away his work from his life, Victor would not know what to do with himself. His only other obsession was his daughter Bharati. One phone call from her and he would fly to Delhi to be with her, even if only for a few hours. Pampered by him—whose absence she often held up as her particular tragedy—and her Dadima, she had become headstrong and self-willed. After changing two schools, neither of which she liked, she refused to join any other, was coached by tutors at home but refused to take any exams. She read a lot on her own and when it came to conversation, could hold her own in any company. She also generally looked down on people. Much of this had to do with her looks. They were unconventional. She was too tall for her age, too thin, and not as fair as other Kashmiri Pandits. Since she spent so much time with her grandmother, she was awkward with forks and knives and wines and cheeses. Her cousins made fun of her table manners and her ill-fitting dresses. She dismissed them as semi-literate fools, though their mockery stung her badly. When provoked too much, she gave them such a tongue-lashing that they avoided her for weeks. She had the sharpest tongue in all of Delhi.

Her aunts got together one evening when the entire family, including Victor, was at Shanti Bhavan and suggested that she be sent to a finishing school in Switzerland. Bharati protested mightily, but they made such a case for it that Victor agreed. She never forgave her aunts for this. She remembered, especially, what one of them had said: 'She needs class. We are too important a family to risk inelegance, bhai.'

Bharati was thirteen when she was sent to a residential finishing school outside Lausanne. The four years she spent there were the unhappiest of her life. She hated the cold, the antiseptic environment and the aloof people. She became cold and aloof herself. Because she had made a promise to her father, she endured it. It helped that Victor made frequent trips to Switzerland to see her. At the end of four years, she packed her bags and returned to Delhi. She was through with formal education; she would have no more of it, even if her Papi said it was his dearest wish that she go to Oxford. 'I am a lady now,' she explained to her father. 'I have class—that much I'll admit Switzerland did do for me. Your sisters need not be embarrassed of me. But no more, Papi. I'll stay here in India, with you.' Victor was stunned that she had been so hurt and he had not realized it. He loved his daughter too much. He gave in. 'I'm sorry, my dear. I had no idea you were so unhappy. Very well, you will live here and there will be no talk of Oxford or further studies.'

Bharati went back to reading, spending time with her Dadima or just lying in her room doing nothing. Although she had grown into a handsome young woman, she took no interest in young men

113

her age. She had no friends nor seemed to want to have any. Her life was going nowhere.

A year after her return from Switzerland, Victor decided it was time father and daughter had a heart to heart talk about their future. He asked her to come to Bombay for a few days, they could go sailing to Goa and Cochin and have time to themselves; they saw so little of each other. 'I would love that,' said Bharati. 'Shanti Bhavan is too crowded for my liking. I could do with a period of quiet to restore my sanity. Sometimes I fear I will go mad here.'

Three days later Victor and Bharati flew to Bombay. Victor spent his days consulting his senior executives and collecting reports and balance sheets of his companies to study on board his yacht. Nair was all over Bharati, loading her with bouquets of flowers and compliments about her looks. Full of self-love that he was, he was struck especially by her sharp nose and sharper tongue, both of which reminded him of himself as a young man. Bharati was not used to being paid attention to by a man, especially one almost the same age as her father, and happily responded to his show of affection.

Victor and Bharati spent a week at sea sailing leisurely down India's western coast, stopping at Goa and Cochin for a day and night either way to refuel and pick up fresh fruit, vegetables, poultry and fish. Victor spent most of his time in his cabin going over the files he had brought with him and writing his comments. Amongst them was a report jointly signed by senior members of his staff that the companies acquire a holiday home somewhere in the hills where they could take their families for vacations, as hotels were too expensive for them. Victor liked the idea, approved it and for good measure added, 'Investigate possibility of acquiring a house on the upper reaches of the Ganga, not very far from Haridwar. The climate should be suitable for summer and winter as a pleasant retreat for any member of our staff who wants a break. Charges should be nominal. Employ a whole-time cook and staff of three. Meals supplied should be strictly vegetarian, in keeping with the traditions of the place.'

At the time he could not have known how important a role the holiday home would play in his life.

Bharati had brought a load of books and magazines with her. She spent most of her time reading on the deck and strolling around the yacht gazing at the coastline on the one side, the open sea on the other. They met at mealtime—briefly for a light lunch, longer for the evening meal. Victor took his quota of two pegs of Scotch and soda. He persuaded his daughter to try out light, dry French wines. In Switzerland she hadn't much cared for wines, here she found them very palatable, both before and with her meals.

When it was time to return to Bombay, Victor finally had the chat he had been meaning to with his daughter. 'I am past fifty now, Bharati. That doesn't make me old, I know, but I am finding the work I have to do too heavy for my shoulders. It leaves me no time to read, write or relax. You are grown up enough to share some of the burden; after all you are my sole inheritor. In retrospect I am glad you did not waste your time going to college and getting degrees or diplomas. They count for very little in life. What counts is work-experience. The sooner you get down to it the better.'

'What do you have in mind?' she asked.

'It won't be a bad idea if you went around all the factories we have. Spend a week or more at every place, examine how it is doing, see if it needs modernizing. We have to be a step ahead of everyone else. Then take a trip abroad. Visit Manchester, Sheffield, Germany, the United States and see if they are producing better goods than ours. A field that needs to be explored is pharmaceuticals. We produce very second-rate material and rely heavily on imports. We are short of power, we need electricity, we must modernize our railways, lay wide roads like they have in Germany and Italy. The list is endless. Start with England. We have a nice, cosy flat in Albion Mews; you can operate from there. Hire a secretary to help you.'

Bharati kept nodding her head in agreement. And while he talked, she visualized the great new world she would be exploring all on her own without anyone keeping an eye on her. She was in for many surprises.

~

Bharati spent the next few months touring India by plane, train and car, visiting all the factories her father had set up. She was well received by the staff and workers, saw the working conditions and heard whatever difficulties they or their families had to face. The workers were impressed by her brisk, no-nonsense manner. She did not talk much but she listened, and promised to apprise her father of any concerns they might have. Her demeanour reminded many of the Prime Minister's daughter who often accompanied her father on his tours through the country. It was true that though Bharati visited their modest homes and walked around like them in chappals in the blazing sun they did not sense the warmth they did with Jai Bhagwan. But then, he was a creature of the sky, a god to them.

Before she finally returned to Bombay, Bharati took time off and spent a week at the holiday home purchased by the company from a local raja on the right bank of the Ganga between Haridwar and Rishikesh. It was being renovated. She was charmed by its setting in the green hills with the gentle roar of the river in the background as it ran over rocks and boulders. It was almost a mile away from the main road going into Tehri Garhwal. Its closest neighbour was a dilapidated ashram run by a woman tantric who was said to own a pet tiger, lots of black dogs and a few disciples. Bharati gave her father a lyrical description of the place over the phone: 'It's the kind of place I would like to spend my life in—river, mountains, lush greenery and peace that passeth understanding. I'll be as happy here as you are on your yacht.' Victor decided to name the holiday home after her, Bharati Bhavan.

While she was away, Victor wrote to his business associates in Europe about his daughter's impending visit and received assuring responses that she would be welcomed and given all assistance possible. Nair suggested that she extend her interests beyond the merely commercial and meet leaders of political parties, visit picture galleries, see plays and ballet programmes and attend classical music concerts. 'She should broaden her horizons,' he said. 'Unofficially she will be a kind of roaming ambassador for India. She should be able to hold her own among the elitest of the elite.' What Nair said made good sense to Victor. Nair added, 'If you like, I will go with her, spend a couple of weeks in London showing her around and introducing her to politicians, poets and writers whom I have known over the years. That will get her started. Thereafter she will be able to handle things on her own.' That also made sense to Victor. 'I'll ask Bharati what she thinks about it,' he said.

Bharati approved of the idea. 'I'll be lost in a strange place without anyone to show me around. Nair would be a great help,' she said.

Her father added a warning note: 'Mind you, he has a very prickly personality. He picks quarrels with people. You'll have to guard yourself against that.'

'I haven't noticed anything prickly about him,' replied Bharati. 'He is always charming and courteous towards me.'

'Don't say I didn't warn you,' said Victor. 'I

have known him since my days in college. I've always been fond of him but few others have.'

Some days later Bharati and Nair arrived in London. Nair, who usually wore his Kerala-style kurta and ankle-length snow-white mundu in India, was turned out in a smart Saville Row suit and a silk tie. Bharati had an expensive shahtoosh shawl draped round her shoulders against London's December cold. Though widely separated by age they made a handsome couple.

Nair was all charm. Every morning he came to pick her up from Albion Mews, carrying a bouquet of red roses and a printed card with the day' schedule: Visit to the Tate Gallery. Lunch at Savoy with the foreign minister. Visit to the Tower of London. Early dinner with the editor of *The Observer*. Theatre to see *Mousetrap* by Agatha Christie . . . The schedule varied every day. He had hired a Rolls-Royce for a fortnight to take them around and then drop him at his digs somewhere near Euston Station which he had kept ever since he passed out of Oxford.

Though he paid Bharati full attention, he was always edgy and impatient to get on to the next item on the day's programme. He barely ate anything at lunch or dinner beside slurping tomato soup and endless cups of tea. London had done something to him: he had become the Nair of thirty years ago. While others ate, he toyed with spoons and forks, pushing the food placed before him from one side of the plate to the other till it was removed untouched. 'Nair, you will die of hunger and cold if you don't have more to eat,' said Bharati to him at one meal and filled his plate with boiled vegetables. He spiked a couple of potatoes with his fork, ate half of each and spat the other half back on the plate. 'Do I look famished to you?' he asked with a ghoulish grin. 'You people eat and drink too much. Remember Gandhi? One glass of goat's milk, a few dates and nuts. He had the energy to take on the British empire at the zenith of its power.'

'He's *always* been like this—ever since I've known him these thirty years,' gushed one of the lady friends he had invited for lunch, 'ask any of his old girlfriends. Everyone wanted to mother him.'

Bharati had heard Nair had many English girl friends, some from rich families who were drawn to his ascetic way of life. They loved to look after him. Bharati, though young enough to be his daughter, also wanted to mother him. Many a time while being driven to places she watched him shiver in the cold and felt a great tenderness for him. 'Your hands are icy!' she said to him in the car one night. 'Here, cover your hands and knees with my shawl, it is the warmest covering in the world.' They shared the shahtoosh and held hands under it. His were bony, like the claws of a predator; hers warm and soft and still forgiving, for she was only a girl yet, barely eighteen.

They were still in London on Christmas Day. The city bore a deserted look. Nair suggested a drive to Eton so Bharati could see the school her father had gone to. It would be closed but they could see the buildings and Windsor Castle. Bharati agreed readily. It would be his last day with her as he was due to fly back to India the next morning and the idea of a long drive with him appealed to her. She had grown fond of this eccentric, indulgent man who gave her so much of his time. It was a sunny day, nevertheless Bharati shared her shawl with Nair and held his hand. She was already beginning to miss him.

By the time they returned it was dark; church bells were tolling for evensong. Bharati lit the gas fire and made a pot of tea for Nair. She took out a bottle of French Beaujolais and put it on the table with the teapot and a plate of salted biscuits. While she was busy Nair was warming his hands in front of the gas fire. 'Feel my hands now,' he said cupping her cheeks, 'warm as toast, as they say.' She came closer to him. He planted a kiss on her forehead.

They sat at the table; he sipping tea and nibbling salted biscuits, she taking gulps of white wine. She rarely took more than two small wine glasses; she was on to her third. After a long day and an empty stomach with only a sandwich for lunch, the wine went to her head. She began to slur in her speech. She noticed him take a quick glance at his watch. 'Youaa in a hurry to get away. Stay. A while longer.'

'Young lady I think you are a little drunk,' he said with a smirk on his face.

'Thathiam,' she lisped. 'I'll lie down for a while. Don't . . . don't you run away.'

She lay down on the sofa-cum-bed. He came and sat by her pillow and brushed her forehead with his claw-like hands. He took the liberty of kissing her on her lips, half expecting to be repulsed. She grabbed his hair and pressed his lips harder against hers. 'Young lady,' he said hoarsely, moving a hand down to her breasts, 'is there anything I can do for you before I go?'

'Make love to me,' she moaned, 'no one has ever made love to me.'

Nair needed no further invitation. He wanted to settle scores with Victor for all the good he had done him. Seducing his teenage daughter would be the ultimate revenge against his benefactor. He proceeded to undress her, then himself, slobbered over her ripe young breasts till she was roused to a frenzy. He entered her. 'Ouch,' she screamed, 'but don't stop.' He did his best. At his best he was not patient enough to fulfil his partner's desires. A few violent thrusts and he was finished. He buttoned his trousers and hurried out of the mews. He laughed maniacally to himself as he emerged on the road outside, startling an old lady walking her dog.

Many Christmases ago her father had lost his virginity on the same sofa-cum-bed to a London whore. Many Christmases later Bharati lost her virginity on the same sofa-cum-bed to a sophisticated but incompetent gigolo.

10

While Bharati and Nair were away in London, Victor suffered a health scare while he was in Delhi visiting his mother. It happened one morning in the shower when a vicious shooting pain in his chest made him all but collapse on the floor. The doctor diagnosed it as angina and assured him that he was in no danger, provided he was careful about his diet and took some exercise and the medicines he prescribed. But Victor was shaken. There was so much to be done still. He was too young to die. A sense of impending doom seized him. He made a will and posted it to his lawyer in Bombay. He found it difficult to concentrate on anything. Perhaps a few days alone in his newly acquired holiday home might help. If it did not work out he could return to Delhi in a few hours. The next day he set off for Haridwar by car with his secretary, cook and bearer following him in another. By noon they passed through Haridwar. Half way on the road to Rishikesh they turned downhill towards the river and reached their destination. Victor was pleased with what he saw: a spacious lawn with flower beds and the white double-storeyed house gleaming in the crisp sunlight. The sight soothed him. The caretaker and gardener touched his feet and escorted him indoors. There was a large reception hall with a part set aside as a dining room, and three sets of bedrooms with bathrooms. A broad staircase led to the upper floor which had another couple of bedrooms and a drawing room opening out into a large open balcony which gave a splendid view of the mountains and the sparkling river flowing in the valley. Victor gazed at the scene in awe and wonder. 'Very beautiful!' he said to the caretaker. 'I should have come here sooner.'

'Yes sir, Raja Sahib used to spend all his evenings gazing at the Ganga till it got dark. He would have never sold this property but for the litigation with his brothers and his state being taken over by the government,' replied the caretaker.

Victor had his afternoon tea in the balcony, looking out at the mountains till his mind was cleansed of every thought. He continued to sit there as the sun went over the hill on which the house stood. A three-day-old moon came up in the dark blue sky close to the evening star. A cool breeze began to blow, carrying on it the undulating notes of a bansuri from some village downriver. The flute melody grew faint and then died down. The scene gradually faded from view. Victor decided to turn in.

Oil lamps had been lit. The caretaker came in to clear the tea tray. 'Sir, there is a power cut. The lights will come on in another hour; I have put a torch on the table by your bedside and a hurricane lantern in your bathroom. I will be sleeping on the ground floor. Just shout for me and I will be at your service.'

Victor's personal bearer laid out a bottle of Scotch and soda and ice for him. The long drive through the country, the fresh mountain air and the music of the bansuri had lifted his spirits. The glow of oil lamps with moths fluttering about and the muffled sound of the rushing river created a very romantic atmosphere. The Scotch went down smoothly, warming him up. He did not brood over the intimation of his mortality that had brought him

127

here. What had to happen would happen, he thought to himself. There was so much beauty in life; how did it matter if in the midst of it there was also death. He only wished he had discovered this place earlier. It had restored him in half a day. After a light supper he climbed into his bed under a mosquito net.

He spent the next two days exploring the countryside and taking long walks along the river bank. He dipped his hand in the fast-running stream and splashed water on his face. It was icy cold. He walked past the ashram Bharati had written to him about, a few hundred yards away from the holiday home. Its gate was closed. On one side of the black metal gate was a crude statue of goddess Durga astride a lion. On the other, a notice in English reading 'No trespassers allowed. Beware of tiger.'

Back home he asked the caretaker about it. 'That, Sir, is the ashram of Ma Durgeshwari. She is a powerful tantric. People say she was born in a cave in the high Himalayas. She owns a tiger called Sheroo who I've been told is a strict vegetarian. He follows her everywhere like a pet dog. She takes him to the Ganga every day and they bathe in the river together. People are scared of going anywhere near them. They call her *Sheron wali ma*—mother of tigers. For her darshan you have to approach her chief disciple who is an Englishwoman.'

Victor saw her early the next morning from his balcony. She was going downhill, the tiger following on her heels. They made an impressive sight. She had a saffron cloth wrapped around her torso and a length of tiger skin around her hips as a skirt. She had a trishul in one hand. Her long raven-black hair was left loose. As she strode down to the Ganga her hair caught the breeze and streamed behind her. The tiger, lean and agile, moved more like a cheetah, looking straight ahead and never once faltering or varying his speed. They got to the river bank where the tantric woman planted the trident she was carrying to indicate that the spot had been reserved for her. She took off the saffron scarf, then the tiger skin. She rolled her hair up and tied it in a bun on top of her head. She was stark naked: skin the colour of old ivory, large, firm breasts and buttocks and a neat black triangular bush between her legs. Victor guessed she would be in her late twenties. For a while she stood rubbing her body with her hands. Then she felt the water, withdrew it quickly and said something to her tiger who raised his long stiff tail once and brought it down slowly. Gingerly she stepped into the ice-cold stream, splashed some water on her body, then sank down into the stream till the water flowed over her head. The tiger jumped into the river and swam up to her side. She splashed water on his face when he came too close to her. They played in the river for a while till she could not stand the cold anymore. She had no towel and exposed her body to the sun to dry her. She sat on a rock, combed her hair with her fingers and re-tied it on top of her head. The tiger licked her body for the drops of water that remained.

They sat in the sun for a while. She covered herself again with the saffron scarf and tiger skin. She pulled out her trident and started uphill towards their ashram. She looked the exact image of Mother India on calendars Victor had seen in paanwala's shops. Suddenly she looked up and saw Victor standing in the balcony. An angry scowl came on her face. She looked away and quickened her pace.

Victor sat back in his chair, exhausted. It had been many years since he had seen a naked woman. He had been busy enough and the lack of sex hadn't really tormented him much. So when he saw the woman bathe in the river he was totally unprepared for the effect it had on him. As he watched her wash her most secret places, he was overcome with violent desire. It was the wild lust that sometimes afflicts the middle-aged and it made him shudder. He was still trembling. He had to get away for a while; he decided to drive out to a nearby town for a surprise check on one of his sugar mills. It would keep him away for a good part of the day.

That evening as he was about to pour himself a second Scotch his secretary came in and announced, 'Sir, Ma Durgeshwari has come to see you. I told her she had made no appointment but she insists she has something of great importance to say and will not take more than ten minutes.'

'Who is she?' asked Victor, knowing full well who she was and the purpose of her visit.

'She is the sadhvi who runs the ashram next door. The one with the tiger.'

'Has she brought her tiger with her?'

'No sir, she is alone.'

'Okay, let her in.'

Victor prepared himself for a dressing down. But not for the kind he got. He heard her come in and latch the door behind her. Without introducing herself she said, '*Ganga mai kay kinaarey baith viskee peeta hai* (You sit by the bank of Mother Ganga and drink whiskey)!'

Victor stood up to greet her and with palms joined mumbled an apology. '*Bhool huee, maaf keejiye*

(It was a mistake, please forgive me).'

'And you stand on top of your big bungalow and watch girls bathing in the nude, *hain*? *Sharam nahin aati* (Aren't you ashamed of yourself)?'

Victor repeated his apology and added, 'It won't happen again.' He hoped that would be the end of the interview and he could resume drinking. Ma Durgeshwari had other ideas. She put her trident against the wall and sat cross-legged on the sofa facing his chair. Her fleshy thighs were exposed. Victor tried to avert his gaze, but it was no use; his mouth was already dry with longing.

'I am told you are the richest man in India and have great ahankaar about your wealth.'

'Yes, Maji, God has been good to me. But I am not arrogant.'

'You talk of God's kindness? I am told you don't believe in God, don't go to temples, don't do any poojas. You think no end of yourself. You are a ghamandi.'

Victor did not contradict her because all that was true. He decided to take the offensive. 'Maji, did you come only to scold me and put me in my place?'

'No, I have much more to say. Although you are a lot older than me, you have not read the Shastras and other holy books. All you have learnt is from the materialistic West where nothing matters more than money. All that is Maya jaal; you must free yourself from that web of illusion. Do you do yoga? Do you meditate? If you do, you will get nearer the truth of life.'

'Maji, I am willing to learn. Please take me on as a disciple.'

'Now you are talking sense. I can tell that you suffer from a sickness. I can cure you. But if you want to be my bhakta you must first touch my feet and seek my blessing.' She uncrossed her legs and put her feet on the ground.

Victor began to enjoy the charade. He went down on his knees and touched her feet. His eyes wandered to her thighs and his hands began to shake. Ma Durgeshwari held his head with both her hands and pulled it to her breast. She untied the sash covering her breasts. 'Now drink the milk from your mother's bosom,' she commanded.

Victor grabbed one soft breast, took it in his mouth and began to suckle it greedily like a hungry babe. He moved to the other and then back to the first one, lapping up the salt of her flesh. Ma Durgeshwari reached down to unbuckle his belt and with her big toes pushed down his trousers. She fondled his testicles and phallus. 'You need release,' she pronounced. Then she took off her tiger skin, lay down on the sofa and commanded: 'Come inside me, but don't move too much.'

Victor entered her and lay still on her with his tongue darting around busily in her mouth. She did not move but by contracting her vaginal muscles began to milk him. Victor had never experienced the sensation with any woman before. His own complete surrender excited him too. Perhaps too much, for soon a shiver of thrill ran through his body as he pumped his hot seed into her, and to prevent himself from howling, clamped his teeth on her shoulder. He lay like a corpse on her. Ma Durgeshwari caressed his face and played with his hair. 'You finish so soon! The fire still burns within me. I'll teach you yoga, you will be able to hold your semen for an hour or more. If you don't want to spill it you can withdraw it within yourself.' Victor raised his head and looked at her, puzzled. She smiled. 'Don't look surprised; it is possible. This is the ignorance I want to cure you of. When I saw you spying on me I knew you had been denying yourself the ultimate in bliss known to mankind. You men only know the quick *chhook, chhook, phut.* Treat sex like worship and you will get more fulfilment than making millions of rupees.'

'Yes, Maji.'

'Arre, what is this Maji business now? You've just fucked me. You know what they call men who do this to their mothers? Call me Durgesh.'

'It is you who have fucked me, Durgesh. And I have no complaints. I've never known sex to be so thrilling, not even when I first did it at fourteen,' said Victor.

'Naturally,' Durgeshwari responded, 'you hadn't met me, so how could you. I've spent years mastering the art of tantra. I will show you things beyond your wildest dreams.'

Victor laughed. 'I don't doubt you will. But be careful with me. My doctor says I should avoid too much excitement, my heart might not be able to take it.'

'Arre these cheer-phaad doctors—what do they know? They cut you up then sew you back and send you to your death before your time. With me you will rediscover your youth. *Solah saal ke chhokre ka dil hoga tera* (You'll have the heart of a sixteen-year-old lad).'

Victor believed every word she said. She had dispelled whatever little gloom still remained in his mind. Sex was the best antidote for the fear of death. 'Will you come to see me tomorrow?' he asked.

135

'I will come as often as you want me.'

'Remember, I have become your bhakta, you can't forsake me,' he said with a grin. 'But don't bring your tiger with you!'

'Sheroo can be very jealous. If he sees you eating me he will eat you up,' she laughed.

He took her in his arms and pressed her middle against his own and ran his hands over her buttocks till he was aroused again.

'Bas, enough!' commanded Durgeshwari. 'Leave something for tomorrow.' She kissed him on his lips.

'The same time tomorrow. I'll send my car to fetch you,' he said.

Early the next morning Victor was on his balcony again, waiting. Ma Durgeshwari and Sheroo appeared soon enough and went down the hillside to the place where they had bathed the day before. Durgeshwari stuck her trident at the same spot and divested herself of her trademark dress. The sight took his breath away all over again.

Before Durgeshwari, Victor had had sex with a few women, mostly whores, and of course his own wife. He was always in a hurry and had little time to savour their bodies before getting down to the act. It had been the same with Durgeshwari when they had made love the previous day. He had barely noticed how perfect she was. Till that morning he had not realized how sensuous a woman's buttocks could be. Most white women's behinds were like men's: two fleshy buns to act as cushions when they sat down. They left Victor cold. His wife's were not much to speak of either. This young sadhvi's, on the other hand, were a delight. They were large and beautifully rounded: if he got the opportunity he would spend hours running the palms of his hands gently over them feeling their contours. Why his ancestors had compared women's buttocks to the hind parts of a female elephant, a hasthini, was beyond his comprehension. Who in their senses would want to stroke the backside of a pachyderm? But here was an apsara rising out of the waters of a holy Ganga, raising her arms in salutation to the sun rising above the range of hills and offering her behind to him to marvel at and worship.

Durgeshwari sensed that she was being watched. She looked up and saw Victor standing on the balcony as she had expected. She raised both her hands high above her head and joined her palms, as if in salutation, showing him all she had to show. He waved back vigorously. What a vision of beauty, he thought. Like Aphrodite rising out of the sparkling waters of the sea. He had never seen a woman as beautiful and free-spirited as this before. Nor any one as hypnotic. He continued to watch her bathe, sport with her tiger and dry herself in the sun. Then she dressed, facing him all the time, went up the mountain path and disappeared from view.

Victor sent for his secretary. 'Go to the ashram and see what it is like. Find out if it is registered as a charitable institution and has a bank account. Take the car.'

Two hours later the secretary returned and reported, 'Sir, it is a ramshackle kind of place with only the office, a Durga temple and a meditation hall which is a pukka building. The rest of the compound has huts with thatched roofs and a shed for three buffaloes. They have a tube well to water their vegetable garden. There are about thirty residents including a swamiji who is their yoga teacher. An Englishwoman who seems to run the show told me it is registered as a charitable institution and they have an account in a bank in Rishikesh. It is a hand-to-mouth existence, sir. In fact they had to give away all their guard dogs because they were too expensive to maintain.'

Victor made out a cheque for one lakh twenty-five thousand in the name of the ashram. In the envelope he also put in a slip in Hindi which read

'Guru dakshina from your latest bhakta', and asked his secretary to put it in the hands of Ma Durgeshwari.

That evening Victor took a long time shaving and bathing—he soaped and scrubbed himself thoroughly, then doused himself with eau de cologne. He brushed his teeth, scraped his tongue and gargled with his specially imported mouthwash. He wore his finest silk shirt and a fresh pair of trousers. It felt good to be young and whole again. He had his bottle of Scotch, soda and bucket of ice laid beside the sofa where he knew he would spend most of his time. He took a large helping of Scotch and waited impatiently for the sound of his car.

He was on his second drink when he heard the car pull up in the porch and hurried down to meet his visitor. As she stepped out of the car, trident in hand, he bent down and touched her feet to show his secretary and chauffeur he was paying deference due to a sadhvi. She let herself be escorted up the stairs. Victor latched the door behind him and took her in his arms. 'Paakhandi (impostor)!' she exclaimed. 'You make chootiyas of your staff? One minute you touch my feet as if I were a devi, the next you put your arms around me lustfully as if I were your rakhail!'

Victor did not contradict her; she was indeed his goddess, his mistress. At the moment she could make him do absolutely anything she wanted. He put away her trident and pulled her close. 'All night and day I have been brooding and waiting for you. I have never felt like this for anyone I've met.'

'Jhootha (liar),' said Durgesh. 'There is no need for such lies. It makes no difference to me how many gori-chitti white women you bedded in vilayat or how many others in India.'

'You are more beautiful than all of them put together. And stop scolding me; the evening is for better things.' He pushed her gently onto the sofa.

'Tell me before you shut my lips: that large sum you sent me this morning, is it in payment for last night or for the ashram?'

'Oh shut up!' snapped Victor impatiently. 'There's only one way to stop you from saying nasty things.' He glued his lips to hers and fumbled with the sash that served as her blouse. She helped him with the task, and as soon as her breasts were free he fastened his mouth to them. Her nipples grew rock-hard against his tongue. 'Lose yourself in your worship,' Durgeshwari urged him, and when his worship had pleased her enough, she pulled his head back. She helped him take his clothes off then undid her tiger skin and said, 'Last night I had half my share of the pleasure due to me. Give me the other half tonight.'

It was a different experience for both. Victor began at her toes and ran his hands from the sides of her feet to her head and his tongue along the inside of her thighs; he bit her breasts, lips and neck. In turn she dug her nails into his buttocks, when he had slid in, urging him to press harder into her. As before, she contracted her muscles and milked him with vigour. He had got used to the sensation and as pleasant as it was he was able to hold back. It was Durgesh who yielded the battle to him. She thrust her hips up with tremendous force and began to moan and then wailed: '*Hai mar gayee* (I am dying). *Qatal kar de* (Kill me)!' Victor raised himself on his arms and toes and gave her all he had, pummelling into her till she thrashed her legs in the air above him and the sofa shook and he felt the room go into a drunken tizzy as if rocked by an earthquake.

It had lasted over an hour. Both were utterly exhausted. Victor released her body from under him. He gave her a gentle kiss on her cheek and said, 'Durgesh, I am in love with you. I can't live without you anymore.'

Durgesh ignored his school-boy confession and replied, 'Look what you have done to me! There are nail and bite marks all over my body. How will I face the people in the ashram? They will think

Sheroo must have attacked me. Are you a man or a tiger?'

'Okay. I am a tiger-man in love with you. Will you marry me?'

'You must be half mad as well. For one you are a Brahmin, I a Kshatriya. We can have sambandh but we cannot be man and wife. For another you must be almost twenty-five years older than me. And most important of all, I am a sadhvi used to living in an ashram. I can't change into a memsahib doing git-pit in English at your parties. So put marriage out of your mind. It is not meant for me or even for you. I will come to you whenever and wherever you want me.'

They no longer talked face to face; he rested his head on her shoulder, his hands caressed her breasts. He kissed them in turns. She squeezed his balls gently and fondled his penis. Thus engaged they talked about their future. He was determined not to let go of her. She was equally determined to hang on to him as long as he could cope with her. 'Tell me, do you do any exercise? Do you know any yoga asanas?' she asked pinching the loose flesh round his stomach. 'You are flabby around your middle. I'll send our Swamiji to you in the morning. He will teach you some asanas, how to breathe properly. He will also teach you how to hold your bindu. It will restore your youth. I don't want my lover growing old before his time. There are many different positions for sex that I want to teach you. You should be fit enough for those.'

~

Swami Dhananjay Maharaj Brahmachari arrived the next morning and he turned out to be another surprise. He was over six feet tall, without an ounce of spare flesh on his body and erect as a soldier at attention. His glossy black hair curled down to his shoulders and his jet-black beard was neatly trimmed. It was difficult to guess his age—he could have been thirty-five, or perhaps forty-five. He was draped in thin see-through one-piece muslin which was both his dhoti and covered his torso. 'Maji told me you want to learn yoga asanas,' he said without a smile.

'Yes Swamiji, Ma Durgeshwari says I am flabby in the middle,' replied Victor patting his stomach. 'Yoga may tone up my system.'

'Let us see. Lie down on the floor.'

Victor lay down on the floor. Swamiji took out a measuring tape from some fold of the white muslin, put one end on Victor's right nipple and measured the distance to his right toe. He did the same from the left nipple to the left toe. 'There is some difference between the two. Do you suffer from gas?'

Victor was taken aback. What kind of question was that for a stranger to ask? Did he imply that he farted too much? 'Some acidity, yes,' he replied uncertainly. 'I get a little wind in the stomach in the afternoons. But it settles down after I have a whisky or two.'

'Gas in the stomach is bad for you. I will teach you a few asanas which will help you get rid of it without drinking whisky. Also the correct way to inhale and exhale. When would you like to start? The best time is in the morning after you have evacuated your bowels. Yoga is best on an empty stomach. And learn to sit properly, like this,' Swamiji sat on the floor and crossed his legs in the lotus pose, padma asana. 'Or like this,' he sat on his legs as tailors and the Japanese do. 'Keep the spine ramrod straight, not curving,' he said.

Victor tried but could not bend his knees appropriately. 'Don't be in a hurry. Try every morning and you'll be able to do it.' Swamiji demonstrated other asanas: standing on one's head—shirsh asana— bending the body like a bow—dhanur asana. Victor watched in complete fascination; Swamiji's body seemed to be made of rubber. 'Breathing properly is most important,' he said resuming the lotus pose. He shut one nostril with his finger and inhaled deeply with the other; then exhaled with a loud hiss. He repeated the inhaling-exhaling through the other nostril. 'But to come back to your particular problem. You tell me you suffer from gas. City-dwellers who spend most of their time sitting in chairs have the same problem. I'll teach you how to exercise your stomach muscles and expel gas out of it.' He churned the muscles of his abdomen till they looked like ripples of waves running down from his chest to his hips. Then he raised his body on both his hands and let out a resounding fart. Victor had to hold back breaking into a guffaw of laughter. Swamiji sensed his discomfort and said, 'Gas is no laughing matter. Please notice, my gas has no smell—it is uttam padvi, of the highest order.' Victor wasn't sure he wanted further demonstration of this kind. But before he could say anything Swamiji was on his back. He bent his legs and pulled them up till his knees were close to his neck. 'Pavan mukta asana,' he said, 'to set the gas free.' This time he farted long and slow, an extended musical note that ended in a melancholic whine. 'Please notice again,' the swami said, 'no smell.' Victor was dismayed. It would be a long session of farts. But the Swami surprised him by swiftly moving onto other asanas—for the spine, the neck, the eyes and the lungs.

The lesson ended after an hour and Swamiji was driven back to his ashram. Victor tried some of the asanas and breathing exercises, broke wind unashamedly and felt his health was improving. When Durgesh turned up in the evening he took her with renewed vigour.

~

Victor had planned to spend only a couple of days in the holiday home. It was already his fourth; and he wanted to prolong the holiday for as long as he could. He had come up to be alone and make terms with mortality. He had hardly thought of his health and possible death since his eyes fell on Durgeshwari bathing in the Ganga. To think of it, he had neglected the two most important things in life: good health and good sex. It was not too late to make amends. At long last he had stumbled on two people who could guarantee him both; he was determined not to let go of them.

He put it to Durgeshwari the next evening after they had finished making love (Ma Durgeshwari had

146

insisted they do it standing up this time, which had both exhilarated and tired him). 'Durgesh, I must return to my business and my family. But now you mean more to me than anything else in the world. I don't want to lose you.'

'You should not even think of losing me; I'll be with you whenever you want me. But I have my ashram, its inmates who rely on me and my Sheroo who regards the ashram as his territory and gets ill-tempered when he is out of his surroundings unless I am with him. You should come here more often. I can come to Delhi if you send a car to fetch me. I've never been to Bombay; I've never seen the sea. I hope you will show them to me.'

'Of course! And don't worry about your ashram. Whenever you are short of money, I'll make a guru dakshina. You've taught me more about life than any guru could have done. I'll take good care of you and your Sheroo. I'll put Swamiji on my pay roll. I think it would be a good idea if you came to Delhi for a few days to meet my mother and daughter. Bring Swamiji with you, there'll be less gossip. He could teach Bharati yoga. She takes no exercise and is very short-tempered. Will you come with me?'

'As long as you make neither a wife nor a

mistress of me,' she replied with a mischievous smile. 'From now on you are our annadaata. You tell us to come to Delhi, we come to Delhi. You tell us *Bumbai chalo*, we go to Bombay. But you and I must both be free, our own persons, always.' Victor gave her his word.

11

The Ganga hurtling down the mountains, Ma Durgeshwari, trishul in hand and followed by her tiger, and Swami Dhananjay Maharaj turned the Europeanized Victor's world upside down. What he had known about his country was from his Anglicized father, seasoned by Gandhi's patriotism. The holy river, the tantric woman and the Swami were the India he had not known. It brought change into a life that was beginning to bore him. He was besotted with the tantric sadhvi; that her response was full-blooded gave him a sense of well-being. Full of new vigour he returned to Delhi after ten days. A couple of days later he sent a large station wagon to fetch Ma Durgeshwari, Sheroo and Swamiji.

His daughter was back from London, more cheerful than she had been for a long time. His mother was happy to learn that he had paid homage to Ganga Mai and become a bhakta of a sadhvi and was practising yoga. Only his sister and her husband were somewhat cynical about his new-found enthusiasm for what he called real India. Victor ignored them.

The cottage once occupied by Valerie Bottomley was got ready for Ma Durgeshwari and Sheroo. A corner room in the large house was prepared for Swamiji. They arrived at tea time. Ma Durgeshwari embraced Victor's mother; Swamiji touched her feet. The staff of the house and their friends hoped to have darshan of the visitors. But the sight of Sheroo sent them scurrying back. Ma Durgeshwari sent word that they should all come back, there was nothing to fear. She would keep her Sheroo chained, if that helped. She asked Victor to arrange for a silver chain, which was done. The devout returned for her blessings. '*Kaatey ga to nahin* (He won't bite, will he)?' they asked. 'If you don't tease him, he is like a pet cat. You must not forget, he too is a very holy being,' Ma Durgeshwari would reply. Bharati was the only person who had no fear of the tiger from day one. She stroked his head; he rubbed himself against her legs. They were like animals of the same species. On the second day, even Victor's mother was persuaded to put her arms round Sheroo's neck; he responded by licking her face. Everyone cheered.

Ma Durgeshwari had arrived with minimum baggage: a small attaché case which contained all her change of clothes—a spare sash to cover her bosom, a saffron lungi to change into—and three copper bowls for Sheroo: one for milk and boiled rice and one for boiled beans and daals, which was his staple diet, and the third for water to drink. While Durgeshwari herself decided to stay with her old habit of sleeping on the floor and spread a tiger skin for the purpose in the bedroom, Sheroo had other ideas. He sniffed around in the cottage and settled himself on a sofa in the main room. This would be his favourite perch.

Victor went to the cottage on the first evening itself. He took Durgesh in a tight embrace and murmured in her ear, 'The three days in Rishikesh were like 300 years in swarg (paradise).'

'*Fillum bahut dekhta hai* (you watch too many movies),' laughed Durgeshwari.

'I haven't seen a Hindi movie in ten years. They are so unreal. My love for you is real. Let's not waste time. Ma is expecting you to join her for dinner; she eats early.'

'I'm not clean. Love-shove will have to wait for another two days. But we can talk love and do other loving things.'

Victor was disappointed but understood. So they settled down to doing other loving things. With merely the sound of her voice, as she described to him the most incredible feats possible in tantra sex, Durgeshwari gave Victor a raging erection. A servant knocked on the door to tell them Maji was waiting for them to join her for dinner. Before they left, Durgeshwari put her hand on Victor's crotch and to his amazement he ejaculated instantly.

At Shanti Bhavan it was a changed dinner table. No plates, forks, knives or cut-glass tumblers. Instead, there were silver thaalis with silver katoris and silver tumblers. The food was saatvik, pure vegetarian, with freshly fried pooris, potato bhaaji, daal, a variety of vegetables, boiled rice and curds, followed by kheer for dessert. Everyone ate with their fingers. Victor did this badly but with great enthusiasm. Bharati seemed to relish the changed menu and dinner etiquette; the Swiss education hadn't wiped out her childhood habits. Victor's mother was most pleased with the change. She even gave Sheroo some pooris; he gulped them down with relish. Only Victor's sister and her ICS husband seemed out of place and hardly ate.

Swamiji was asked to conduct yoga classes: in the mornings at home for the family and servants, in the evenings in the business premises for the office staff. Victor attended both and had the enthusiastic support of his daughter who did the same, because she could see that it was doing her Papi good and she wanted to ensure that he stayed with it. After a week of practice Victor was able to sit in the lotus pose and do the headstand with the help of Swamiji. Bharati being much younger and more supple did not find it too hard to master the simpler asanas. Swamiji paid special attention to the young daughter of his benefactor, correcting her posture, and the angles of her hands and legs. Sometimes he let his hands rest for longer than necessary on her legs and hips, so much like a boy's. He was strongly attracted to this lean, tough-looking girl. There was something distinctly masculine about her aura that added to her unusual beauty. What would it feel like to have her long legs wrapped around his, he wondered. But he wasn't a rash man. He wouldn't risk disrepute and the loss of Jai Bhagwan's patronage. Besides, she intimidated him—though this too excited him. He thought it best to concentrate on being a good yoga teacher for the moment.

Both Victor and Bharati were happy with Swamiji

and agreed that it would be a good idea to engage him as a yoga instructor for their companies on a good salary and have him visit their mills and factories by rotation. They put the proposition to Ma Durgeshwari. 'So you're going to steal Swamiji from me, hain?' she smiled. 'I don't mind, provided you make sure he spends at least four months of the year with us in the ashram. That is where he belongs.'

Swamiji was overjoyed. His life's mission to take the message of yoga to the whole of India would be fulfilled. And he would save enough to live in comfort for the rest of his days.

Thus Ma Durgeshwari, Sheroo and Swami Dhananjay Maharaj Brahmachari became an integral part of the Mattoo family. Even Victor's sisters and their families reconciled themselves to the change.

The only one who did not approve of the new entrants into the charmed circle was Nair. He had been elected to Parliament as a Congress candidate and divided his time between Delhi and Bombay. In both places meeting Victor was becoming increasingly difficult; he was frequently busy with his new friends. When he finally got some time alone with Victor, he did not mince his words. 'Victor, who are these weirdos you've got into the family? I am told there's a naked lady who carries a spear and rides a tiger.

And a bearded fellow who teaches people how to stand on their heads. Are you going nuts?'

'Maybe I am,' Victor laughed. 'You meet them and you'll also go nuts. The kind of education we had can be very limiting. You shouldn't have a closed mind. You've become a black Englishman.'

'Good of you to remind me who I am,' sneered Nair. 'I prefer to walk on my legs than on my head. And I really don't need to know the right way to break wind, thank you very much.'

He was more disappointed with Bharati's reaction. He assumed he had established the right to reprimand her. 'What are you doing with this savage with long hair and black beard? I am told he is teaching you how to contort your body in weird postures. You're being a bloody idiot, young lady.'

'Watch your mouth, Nair,' she snapped. 'Swamiji's a wonderful yoga teacher and the most wonderful man I have met. You won't understand him because he speaks only Hindi—India's national language, I might remind you. You can't say a single sentence in Hindi. But for the blind support our mill workers gave you, you would not have got into the lavatory of the Parliament House Annexe.'

Nair was taken aback. Was this the same girl he had deflowered only some months ago!

'Bitch!' he hissed with all the venom he had in him.

She glared at him with her large eyes and said in a cold, even voice, 'You repeat that word and I'll slap you across your beggar's face. Now get out!'

~

A month later, workers of Jai Bhagwan Textiles in Bombay, the biggest of the company's many ventures, went on a day's strike with the threat that if their demands were not met they would close down the mill. Victor asked Nair to meet them and discuss their demands. Nair expressed his inability to do so as the mill workers were in his constituency and there would be clash of interests. He further suggested that since Bharati was to take over charge in due course of time, she should get experience of labour problems. Victor agreed and asked Bharati to look into the matter. Bharati did her homework. She got figures of salaries paid by other mills and compared them with those of Jai Bhagwan Textiles and the extra benefits provided for them. She called a meeting of workers in the mill compound. She took Swamiji with her because all of them attended his yoga sessions. Dressed in a simple grey cotton sari, her head covered with the pallu, she sat on a platform behind a table with a microphone. Swamiji sat beside her. Another microphone was put up on an adjoining table for the workers' representative. There were several thousand workers and their wives in the assemblage. Bharati opened the proceedings with a short speech. '*Bhaiyon aur behno*, I am told you have some grievances against the company. I want you to tell me what they are and I will try to sort them out for you right here. Let me hear what they are.'

A man got up and came to the second microphone. He had a sheaf of papers in his hand. 'Madam Bharatiji,' he started after clearing her throat. Bharati interrupted him. 'Please first introduce yourself. Which section of the mill are you working in?'

'I am not a mill worker, I am the leader of a trade union which represents workers of many mills in Bombay including yours. I want to present our demands—'

Bharati interrupted him again. 'I don't want to hear you; I want to hear what our own workers have to say. Please, brothers and sisters, don't you have anyone amongst you to tell me what is wrong?' She held aloft a sheet of paper and continued, 'Here I have figures of salaries paid by us and those paid by other mills. With benefits like free housing, free medical services, free schooling for your children and annual paid holidays, what we give you is almost twice as much as other mills. You have been lied to. I am like your sister, and it hurts me that my own brothers and sisters should trust an outsider more than me and my father. Please tell me who has put you up to this mischief. Together we will—'

The union leader cut her short and shouted into the microphone: 'You will allow this spoilt brat of your exploiter insult one of your own? This chit of a girl dares to call me a mischief maker! I will teach her a lesson she won't forget for the rest of her life. I will . . .'

Bharati shot up and spread her arms out towards the crowd of workers. 'Brothers, will you sit and watch your younger sister be threatened? I know what kind of lesson he means to teach me. Will you tolerate such vulgarity, my brothers!'

There was an uproar. One of the workers stood up and shouted at the union leader: 'Stop this bakwas and get out of our mill compound at once! Or we will give you such a thrashing you will spend the rest of your life as an invalid.' He raised both his hands and shouted, 'Bharati Behn', and the crowd yelled back, 'Zindabad!' The union leader made a hasty exit, making obscene gestures with his hands.

A group of workers, among them some women with chappals in their hands, chased after him. Bharati had won the first round hands down and gave her father a detailed account of what had transpired. He patted her on the shoulder and said, 'Shabaash. You've made me proud.'

Three days later the weekly tabloid *Thunder*, published in English, Marathi and Hindi, devoted most of its pages to the confrontation between Bharati and the union leader. The banner headline read, 'Tycoon's Daughter Insults Respected Trade Union Leader.' There was a detailed account of how he had not been allowed to present the workers' case, had been threatened, abused and forced to leave the meeting. It also had pictures of Jai Bhagwan's home in Delhi, Jai Bhagwan Towers and his yacht, alongside pictures of workers' quarters. The caption read: 'How the boss lives. And how his slaves live.' There was a boxed item showing salaries, benefits and board meeting fees drawn by the directors. Nair's name was not on the list. The editor of *Thunder* who lived in considerable style on Malabar Hill was a close friend of Nair's. The significance of this wasn't lost on Victor and Bharati.

Swamiji read the Hindi version of the issue. While breakfasting with Victor, Ma Durgeshwari and Bharati, he remarked blandly, '*Kisi namak haraam ke kaam lagta hai* (It looks like the work of someone untrue to his salt).' No name was mentioned.

Soon afterwards, Swami Dhananjay left to spend three months at the ashram in Rishikesh. Ma Durgeshwari followed, promising Victor that she would be back soon. Victor waited impatiently and this time on her return extracted a promise that she wouldn't stay away for longer than a month at a stretch. And so it came to be that the tantric god-woman, the tiger and the yoga teacher spent several months a year in Bombay. There were times when all five of them happened to be staying in the upper floors of Jai Bhagwan Towers. Ma Durgeshwari and Sheroo occupied the guest rooms in Victor's penthouse apartment overlooking the city and the bay where *Jal Bharati* was often anchored. The floor below was occupied by Bharati. The one below hers was divided into two flats—one was alloted to Swamiji, the other permanently reserved for Nair who used it whenever Parliament was not in session and he came down to Bombay. By now he knew that he had become an unwanted outsider. He saw Victor only when he had to and barely nodded in reply to Ma Durgeshwari's greetings, always adding in English, 'Please keep that animal away from me.' He completely ignored Bharati and refused to as much as look at her when she came in to see her father at the office. His resentment was focused on Swamiji. He had no doubt the athletic clown had replaced him as Bharati's lover: he was younger and handsomer than he and evidently adept at other exercises besides yoga. Swamiji treated Nair with the generous condescension usually reserved for a defeated rival. One day he walked into Nair shouting at the security guard at the building gate and said, 'Nair sahib, *aap mein krodh bahut hai* (You have a lot of anger stored up inside you). It's like constipation; yoga can help you overcome both.' Although Nair could not speak Hindi he understood the word krodh and snapped back in English, 'Mister yogi man, I can deal with my krodha and my constipation. I don't have to stand on my head to get the better of them. Thank you.' Swamiji didn't quite understand what had been said, but Nair gave him a look of such contempt that thereafter the swami avoided talking to him.

The strain took a toll on Nair's nerves. He decided to bring matters to a head by having a heart-to-heart talk with Victor. He assumed he had a major role in making Victor the pioneer that he was and Jai Bhagwan Enterprises the most prosperous in the country. In his own eyes he was indispensable.

He ran into Victor in the lift which serviced only the top three floors. 'I want to have a serious talk with you, Victor—but with no one else around. You know who I mean.'

'I too want to have a talk with you,' replied Victor. 'I've been wanting to do so for quite some time.' He looked at his watch. 'It's 9.30 now, make it 10. I promise there'll be no one else around.'

Nair went up to Victor's penthouse. He could smell the tiger; clearly that barbarian and her beast had been in the room a few minutes earlier. Clearly they'd been fucking each other senseless. Quite likely the tiger had joined in and humped them both. Nair did not bother to sit down.

'Look Victor, I don't like the way things are going,' he said bluntly. 'I don't understand your new friends. It is for you to decide whether you want me around as advisor as I have been now for almost thirty years or this grotesque lot you and Bharati have picked up. I'm saying this for your own good.'

Victor was equally blunt in his reply, though he sounded weary, as if being forced to say something unpleasant. 'I agree we've worked together for many years without there being any misunderstanding between us. But I have a feeling you'd rather be on your own. Your political career is more important to you. I understand that. Let there be no ill feelings between us. We can part as friends.'

This was not what Nair had expected to hear. For some time he sat back in his chair holding his head in his hands as the truth sank in: he was being fired. He felt wronged, betrayed and humiliated. A violent rage built up in him and soured his gut. He would teach this pampered upstart and his bitch of a daughter what it was to trifle with a man like him. He got up abruptly and said, 'Right. I will send in my resignation today. Best of luck to you and your menagerie.'

Much as Victor tried not to think of Nair, the manner of their parting bothered him deeply. He brooded over it all morning; it disturbed his afternoon nap. While having tea he told Durgeshwari and Bharati who in her turn told Swamiji. Durgeshwari's only response was, 'He did not like me or my Sheroo. I don't think he likes anyone except himself.' Then she lit a bundle of incense sticks, put them in a vase facing the idol of Durga astride her lion and said a short prayer invoking her protection for her benefactor. Swamiji was more forthright. '*Bura aadmi hai* (He's a bad man). His tongue is coated with venom. He has a big ego, bad temper and desire for revenge. Please be careful of

163

him.' Bharati bit her lip without making any comment.

~

Till Nair's departure Bharati's relations with Swamiji were those of a disciple and teacher. She was attracted to him but wasn't about to make the first move till she could be sure about Swamiji's feelings towards her. Perhaps he really was sworn to celibacy as all the yogis and Matas were supposed to be. So she chose discretion over adventure and quietly looked forward to her yoga lessons and enjoyed the silken touch of his large, gentle hands as he corrected her posture. She wished he would take more liberties with her but he remained covert in his behaviour. One day he came in for her private lessons looking a little uncertain. Bharati noticed instantly that he wasn't wearing anything underneath his lungi. The shadow of his penis swayed like a heavy pendulum behind the thin muslin as he walked towards her. Bharati smiled to herself. 'You have learnt almost everything I could teach you,' he said. 'All you need to do now is to continue doing the yoga asanas I have taught you.'

Bharati was dismayed. 'No, no Swamiji, I need your guidance every day or I will give up these

164

exercises. I am like that, no discipline. Besides, my father tells me I am short-tempered. I am sure you can do something about that.'

Swamiji thought over the matter for a while, brushed his beard with both his hands and ordered, 'Lie on your back.' Bharati did as she was ordered. 'I'll see what is wrong.' He took out his tape measure and proceeded to measure the distance between her navel and each of her big toes.

'My father told me you measure him from his nipples to his toes. Why this gender difference?'

Swamiji brushed his beard again and replied, 'Because Indian women do not like strange men touching their breasts. Also, women's breasts are of different sizes: some are very small, others very big; some are taut and erect, others droop down to their naabhees. I can never be sure.'

'Well, mine don't droop to my navel so your measurements should be possible. And I don't mind you touching my breasts. After all, you are my guru. Besides, you are not allowed to *know* a woman, are you?' Without waiting for his response she sat up, took off her blouse, undid the strap of her bra, pulled it off and lay down again. Swamiji touched her nipples, still holding the rope in his fingers. Her nipples became hard. They were like rivets. 'You have very beautiful breasts,' he said. 'Beautifully rounded and taut.' He stroked them gently with his hands. 'Like an apsara's.'

'Kiss them,' she ordered.

Swamiji kissed them in turn—once, twice, twenty times. He could not believe his luck.

'Put that thing hiding in your lungi inside me,' she ordered again, as she pulled up her sari and spread out her thighs to him. He came over, flicked the flap of his lungi aside to reveal his engorged penis and entered her. She uttered a loud 'Ha!', clutched his long hair and put her lips to his. His beard brushed her breasts as he gently heaved in and out of her body. 'This is heaven,' she murmured in his ears. 'So it is said in our holy books. A maithun between lovers is the closest you can get to the divine in human life,' he replied and speeded up, his breath building up to match precisely the rhythm of his thrusts.

Bharati came once, then a second time, shuddering and gurgling thickly, and lay back utterly exhausted and fulfilled. Swamiji did not spill his semen in her and took out his member still erect and put it behind his lungi.

Bharati put the memory of her brief pathetic encounter with Nair out of her mind as if it had never happened.

12

Over the next six months, Victor involved Bharati, now twenty-one, in most aspects of his several businesses. Nair was busy in Delhi trying to salvage his reputation: in a rare instance of misjudgement, he and a senior minister had vociferously championed the case of communist China even as several other politicians and the chiefs of the armed forces were warning about possible aggression. After the brief but devastating Chinese invasion caught the country unawares, Nair became a laughing stock. He was now working overtime to get back into the good books of the Congress leadership. At Jai Bhagwan Enterprises this meant peace. Victor and Bharati and their senior staff worked well together and efficiency improved. The company's generous contributions to the war efforts had also won it considerable goodwill. Things couldn't have been better.

It was around this time that the head of the public relations department which was under Bharati's charge came to see her about a peculiar problem. 'Madamji,' he said, 'there's a man from *Thunder* who wants us to place ads in his tabloid. I told him it is our policy to place ads only in national newspapers, not in local tabloids. But he is very insistent and says he will make it worth our while to do so or we may have to regret our decision. He wants to see you.'

'Send him in, I will talk to him alone,' replied Bharati. The man was ushered in: small, dark, holding his hat against his chest. He bowed several times before Bharati.

'Yes,' said Bharati in as matter-of-fact a voice as she could, 'what is it you want to say?' She did not ask him to sit down.

'Madam-sir, we have information about the backgrounds of Ma Durgeshwari and Swami Dhananjay Brahmachari which will damage your company's reputation. My editor is willing to withhold its publication if madam-sir will agree to place ads in our paper on a permanent basis.'

Bharati gave him a long, cold stare and hissed, 'Blackmail. How dare you. Get out at once!' She rang the bell. As her chaprasi came in she ordered, 'Take a good look at this man. Remember his face. Throw him out of the office and never let him in again.'

The next issue of *Thunder* had pictures of Victor with Ma Durgeshwari and Bharati with Swami Dhananjay Maharaj on its front page and a lurid account of the background of the tantric and the yoga teacher. According to the tabloid's special correspondent and his research team, Ma Durgeshwari's real name was Shanti Devi; she had been thrown out by her husband in Jhansi who suspected adultery, and had lived with three other men who all ditched her before she became a sadhvi. She had now found a patron in India's richest man, Swamiji also had an earlier incarnation as Durga Das, one of the many sons of an impoverished farmer, a school dropout who had twice been up before a juvenile court on charges of thieving and buggery. He had picked up yoga in a borstal and was now teaching yoga asanas to workers of Jai Bhagwan industries including Kumari Bharati Devi, the only heir to her father's vast fortune.

Victor did not tell Durgeshwari about the

scandalous report; she never read any papers. Nor did Bharati tell Swamiji about it. He read only Hindi; they had not received the Hindi edition of the tabloid. But Bharati spoke to her father. 'This is plain and simple libel. We could take that bastard of an editor to court for heavy damages.'

Victor smiled and replied, 'Don't be childish. There is nothing in the paper against either of us except that the two are our friends. Just throw the rag in the dustbin and forget about it.'

'Who do you think is behind it? I can't think of anyone except Nair.'

'I don't think he'd sink so low. It was just an attempt at blackmail which flopped.'

Many journalists wanted to pick up the story and asked for appointments with Victor and Bharati. Both refused to see them. However, *Thunder* paid a heavy price for launching the smear campaign against Jai Bhagwan Enterprises. Many companies which supplied Jai Bhagwan raw materials or had outlets for sales of his products withdrew advertisements from *Thunder*. So did many state governments and ministries of the central government. Its circulation went down steeply. Jai Bhagwan was too big a person to be trifled with; he had become a national icon and a role model for future generations. The

Times of India carried a front page editorial in his defence. Without naming *Thunder* it alluded to the growth of yellow journalism, rampant trade unionism which was killing many industries and irresponsible politicians who misled workers to go on wildcat strikes. It wrote about what the country owed to Jai Bhagwan in making it self-sufficient in textiles, sugar, steel, cement, pharmaceuticals and much else. For good measure, it reminded people of how much he had done for the nation during the recent war. The editorial concluded with the words 'those who spit at the sky have the same spit fall on their face.'

The smear campaign died out. Only to be replaced by an alarming increase in anonymous letters, hate mail and demands for money. Sending unsigned letters about the private lives of men and women working in the same establishment was a national pastime. Every time someone was appointed or promoted there would be a few letters insinuating that the appointee or the appointee's spouse had obliged some member or the other of the governing body to secure the post. Victor had grown used to them by now. He enjoyed reading them but never took any of them seriously. There were others in different languages full of abuse for him and members of his family. Victor read them as well, smiled to himself and tore them up and threw them in the waste-paper basket. There were a third lot ordering him to deliver a packet of currency notes at a particular time and place to someone who would be waiting there for him. If it was not done one of his mills would be set on fire, or worse, his daughter would be abducted. The mill part did not bother Victor too much, but Bharati was all he had of his own flesh and blood and he was not willing to take any chances with her safety. She often went out shopping on her own and sometimes took a brisk walk along Marine Drive from Chowpatty to Nariman Point. Many people recognized her. He did not think reporting the matter to the police would help; the Bombay police was known to be in cahoots with the underworld. Without telling Bharati he deputed his most senior security guard to follow her wherever she went and inform him when she returned home. Her safety began to weigh on his mind, especially since she was too proud and too much of a daredevil to take any precautions herself.

~

Victor and Bharati were in Delhi when his mother, close to eighty, heavily diabetic and almost blind, had a fall. She went into a coma and never recovered.

Victor was sitting by her pillow holding her hand when she breathed her last. She was cremated the same evening. And as had happened after his father's death, the entire family took the ashes to Haridwar to be immersed in the Ganga. This time, on Bharati's insistence, Victor had his head shaved. Instead of returning to Delhi he persuaded the family to spend a few days at the holiday home. In the evening he sent his car to fetch Ma Durgeshwari from the ashram.

Durgeshwari did not take Sheroo with her as she had other things on her mind for the evening. She saw Victor's shaven head and understood what had happened. 'Om Namo Shivaya, Om Namo Shivaya,' she intoned loudly. 'So Mataji has attained swargvaas. She will find a special place beside Lord Shiva's lotus feet.' They sat in silence for some time. She saw tears well up in Victor's eyes and run down his cheeks, and Bharati and her aunts sniffle and blow their noses in their dupattas. 'It is not proper to cry over the death of a person who has lived a full life and attained nirvana. It should be a cause for celebration,' she admonished them. Her words were soothing. She stayed till it was time for the evening prayers. Before leaving she said, 'Tomorrow morning we will have a special pooja in the ashram for the peace of her soul.

You must all come on your way back to Delhi.'

They stopped by at the ahram for the pooja. Victor saw that the guru dakshina he had offered had been put to good use. In addition to the temple and the meditation hall, all rooms meant to house the bhaktas were pukka structures as well. They had employed a gardener: the vegetable patch had been doubled, there were flowers on either side of the path from the gate, and bougainvillea creepers covered many walls with deep mauve, pink and white. The number of bhaktas seemed to have increased.

The pooja lasted half an hour. Ma Durgeshwari chanted Sanskrit shlokas in a deep, hypnotic voice that made the skin on Victor's and Bharati's arms come up in gooseflesh. As the chanting rose to a crescendo, the Englishwoman at the ashram went into a frenzy and fell at her tantric guru's feet and thrashed about like a fish out of water. After the aarti, Ma Durgeshwari helped the woman up gently and blessed her.

As the family were about to get into their cars, Ma Durgeshwari sidled up to Victor, 'I want to be with you for a few days while you are in Delhi. Will you send a car to fetch me tomorrow or the day after?'

Victor nodded. 'After the chautha ceremony, as

soon as two of my sisters leave. The third stays in the house with her husband.'

The stream of mourners abruptly ended with the chautha. Bharati left for Bombay, Victor's two sisters left for their homes; the ICS brother-in-law and his wife decided to go to Calcutta to see his parents. Victor sent a car to fetch Durgeshwari.

They had the house to themselves, but for the sake of abundant caution Victor put up his guest in Valerie's cottage. Besides, it was more cosy and lived in and altogether a better place for making love than the large mansion. Victor had his personal servant put Scotch, soda and ice and his cut-glass tumblers on a table in the small sitting room. Durgeshwari had never objected to his drinking. At times she took a sip or two from his tumbler. 'Let me taste this stuff you like so much,' she said again. 'Uffo, it has no taste—runs down my throat like fire water. But it gives me a little suroor. It's a nice feeling before maithun.'

They made love. She was gentle and slow. She mothered him because he had lost his mother. 'I'll teach you something new,' she said between long bouts of kissing. 'We will lie on our sides, facing each other. I will guide you in and you must stay inside me without getting too excited. Don't think of women you have made love to or want to make love to; empty your mind of all thoughts. I will milk you. Preserve your bindu so you can do it again and again.' So they lay entwined in each others arms, his hands fondling her breasts. 'I am tired,' she said at last as she gently pushed him out of her and went down to kiss his phallus, still hard and erect like a bamboo pole. Victor felt strangely calm and on top of the world.

They repeated the exercise three evenings running. Each time Victor emerged from her body more triumphant, buoyant and lighter of step. His mind was clearer, he worked harder and went out of his way to exchange pleasantries with everyone he met. He wished it could go on for ever.

Alas, all good things must come to an end. So did his newfound prowess and pride in his body. Early one morning he received a call from Bharati. 'Papi, a section of our textile mill caught fire last night and has been totally destroyed. Three workers lost their lives.' She sounded remarkably in control. 'I am going there straightaway to find out what happened. Come as soon as you can.'

Victor was concerned for her safety. 'Bharati, you don't need to go there yourself. I am sure the general manager can handle things. Have you informed the police?'

'Yes, yes, Papi,' she replied. 'The GM is there. Also the police. The union is organizing a demonstration against the management. I must be there. You come as soon as you can.'

Victor told Durgesh. 'I will not let you go alone; I am coming with you,' she said firmly.

They took the next flight to Bombay. The mill's GM and a few police officers were at the airport. The GM filled Victor in on the details. 'Sir, the situation has taken a nasty turn. After the cremation of the workers who were killed in the fire, workers of other mills have gone on strike and are organizing demonstrations outside your mill.'

The mill was on the way from the airport to Jai Bhagwan Towers. The police advised him to take a different route. Victor ignored their suggestion. 'I will go to the mill right now. Where is my daughter?'

'Sir, despite our pleading with her, she is at the mill. We have provided her adequate security.'

Victor and Ma Durgeshwari drove up to the mill. There was a large crowd outside. A phalanx of policemen armed with lathis faced a mob of mill workers squatting on the road. The police cleared the way and opened the gates to let Victor's car enter the mill. Bharati met them just inside the gate, her face flushed with anger.

'It was done by outsiders,' she said fiercely. 'I've spoken to our workers, they swear they had nothing to do with it. "Kill our own mai-baap, our own annadaata—we are not mad," they say.'

'Then who? And why?' asked Victor. 'And who are those outsiders on the road?'

'They are members of some union or the other. The fellow who was leading them last time is leading them again.'

Victor asked the police to allow workers of the mill to come in so he could talk to them. The officer in charge was hesitant at first but Victor insisted: 'They are my people, I have nothing to fear. Please do as I say.' The policeman relented and made the announcement on the megaphone. Workers were checked and came in an unending line. They bowed to Victor and sat down on the ground.

Victor spoke to them. 'Have you any grievances against the management?' he asked.

The question was answered by silence.

He pointed to the charred remains of the burnt-out section and continued, 'We, that is you and I, will rebuild this part of the mill. We will never be able to bring back to life three of our fellow workers who perished in the fire and we will all have to live with that for the rest of our lives. I know I will and

I don't need to prove it to you after all these years. You will either believe me or you won't. On behalf of the management I announce a compensation of rupees one lakh each to members of the bereaved families. We will also give employment to their widows or sons in the mill.'

There were loud shouts of 'Jai Bhagwan ki Jai.'

'If you wish to hear what the leader of the demonstrators outside has to say I will invite him here to speak to you.'

There was a murmur of assent. Victor asked the inspector of police standing by his side to go and ask the union leader if he wanted to speak to the workers. The union leader walked in jauntily and took the microphone. 'Bhaiyon aur beheno—we are all fellow workers. Our interests are common. We . . . '

Victor interrupted him. 'You don't work in any mill. Tell them the truth.'

'Jai Bhagwan, you wanted me to speak, so don't interrupt me,' the leader said curtly and went on: 'As I was saying, our interests are common. We have to stand united against capitalists who exploit us. You know the slums and hovels we have to live in. Have you seen the palatial mansions these people live in with hordes of servants? Your proprietor even has a

179

ship of his own where he spends his days and nights so he does not have to see how the poor of Bombay live. It is there he entertains his friends, including the half-naked sadhvi lady you see sitting on the dais beside him. No personal offence meant,' he said turning to Victor and Durgeshwari.

At the mention of Durgeshwari Victor's composure snapped. He saw red and he did something completely out of character. He sprang up from his chair like a cheetah and planted a stinging slap on the union leader's face that sent him reeling off the dais. A roar went up in the crowd of workers. A police officer blew his whistle; policemen came rushing in to help the union leader get up. He was led away shouting obscenities—'Haraamzaada, maaderchode—what does he think of himself! Bhainchode—you will soon learn what it is to hit a worker's leader!'

Someone from the crowd shouted, 'Why did you do that, sahib? All for that manhoos sadhvi? She means more to you than us? She is evil; she will destroy you.'

Victor rushed down the dais and into the crowd, 'Who said that? Come out and face me!' he thundered. There was a stunned silence. No one had seen him in such a rage. Bharati came up and led him away by the arm. 'Come away, Papi. These people don't deserve you.'

They went back to Jai Bhagwan Towers in complete silence. There was little talk when they reassembled in Victor's sitting room. 'I should not have hit that bastard; I've never hit anyone in my life. I don't know what came over me.'

'Lose your temper and you lose the argument,' said Durgeshwari softly. 'However, what happened has happened. Let's see what comes next.'

'I can guess,' replied Victor. 'The press will gun for me. The fellow will take me to court for assault and battery. I will become India's villain number one.'

'After all you've done for the country?' asked Bharati. 'Don't worry, it will soon blow over.'

Ma Durgeshwari was quiet. She had made a decision.

Victor had little sleep that night. The more he thought over the matter, the more he was convinced that Nair was behind the union agitation and the campaign that *Thunder* had launched against him. He may not have had anything to do with the fire at the mill, but Victor wasn't entirely sure anymore. It was true that Nair had goaded him to think his vision for India through all those years ago and helped in publishing his book. But then Victor had given Nair a career, made him the highest-paid executive in the country, helped him to get elected to Parliament from a constituency in which no one could speak Malayalam and few understood English. Why should Nair turn against him? He had heard someone say that you do good to anyone and you make an enemy for life. He had refused to believe it then but now thanks to Nair he was coming round to accepting that point of view.

Yet, Victor argued with himself, he must not let his experience of Nair sour him against his countrymen. They had expressed their gratitude to him in more ways than one. Some had reservations about his lavish style of living in a poor country. He felt he had earned it by his own sweat. Perhaps *Jal Bharati* was an extravaganza but it was now his haven of refuge from people with whom he had very little in common. After Nair's turn around he felt he needed his floating little island off the shores of his country more than ever before in his life. He kept reminding himself he must not let people like Nair, the editor of *Thunder* and the professional rabble-rouser calling himself a union leader make him cynical. Lines from the Bhagwad Gita Bapu Gandhi had once asked him to memorize came back to him:

Karmanye ev adhikaraste, ma phaleshu kadachana—
Your right is to do the work assigned to you, not count the fruits of the reward. He muttered the lines softly, over and over, and felt more at peace with himself.

He got up early and sent word to the others that he was going to spend a few days on his yacht. If anyone wanted to come along they were welcome. They agreed it was a good idea. They left Jai Bhagwan Towers well before sunrise. Only early morning walkers were out on Marine Drive. They picked up the morning papers from a stall near the Gateway of India.

As they waited for *Jal Bharati* to pull up near the steps, Victor scanned the headlines. He was right, he had made the first page in all of them. They also carried interviews with the union leader who confirmed that he was taking Victor to court for criminal assault. Victor was sure that *Thunder* would fill its pages with pictures of his entourage and lurid stories about their private lives. He was not going to see it. And being out in the open seas no journalists would pester him for interviews. He would let his PR department handle them as best as it could.

Victor did a lot of walking round the deck and clearing his mind of confusion. He was convinced that the best way of doing things for his country and its people was to maintain a respectable distance from both. Distance lent objectivity and a clearer perspective; closeness made you aware of warts and blemishes—there were far too many of those and they made everything look ugly and repulsive. Buying *Jal Bharati* had been a splendid idea. It gave him the unique privilege of being both in India and away from it. The motor boat which brought fresh water and provisions also brought some senior executive or the other with files which needed to be cleared urgently. Work did not suffer. It was an ideal arrangement. He would soon make *Jal Bharati* his permanent base.

His mind made up, he returned to Bombay. He had to stay there till the burnt-out section of his mill was rebuilt and functional again, which would take a few months. He would let Bharati handle the details.

Meanwhile, he made enquiries about the outcome of the union leader's complaint against him. The police had refused to entertain his first information report (FIR) and told him to file a case through a lawyer if he wanted to do so. There was little hope of the man getting anything more out of it. So he dropped the matter and vented his spleen against

Victor and the police in the press. Only *Thunder* supported him; all important newspapers and magazines wrote favourably about Victor and Jai Bhagwan Enterprises.

Frustrated, the union leader finally turned to Nair who owed him much for the workers' votes which had put him in Parliament. Nair wanted to get even with Victor, his daughter and their new friends. He put in a vaguely worded question to be answered by the minister of labour—a post he himself had wanted—about the recent unrest among factory workers and the repressive measures adopted by the police to put it down. When the question came up, the minister simply replied, 'A statement has been laid on the table of the House.' The statement flatly denied any workers' unrest anywhere in the country. Nair rose to ask supplementary questions, quite forgetting in his excitement that the minister was his own party colleague. He waved a copy of *Thunder* and shouted, 'The honourable minister says there is no trouble anywhere. I draw his attention to this weekly journal which reports incidents of violence in the biggest textile mill in Bombay. A respected trade union leader was insulted and assaulted by the owner of the mill. The capitalist press maintained a conspiracy of silence. Only one progressive paper had the courage to tell the truth.' He walked down the aisle and handed a copy of *Thunder* to the minister. From the back of the House some member shouted: 'Namak haraam!'

Nair stopped in his swaggering march towards his seat and shouted, 'Who dares to call me namak haraam?'

Three voices responded, 'You are a namak haraam. Not only do you attack your own party colleague, you have also stabbed your benefactor in the back. How many years did you eat Jai Bhagwan's salt?'

The opposition benches protested on behalf of Nair. They were enjoying this. The speaker stood up and said, 'Namak haraam is unparliamentary. It will not go on record.'

Nair was visibly upset. As he got back to his seat, he addressed the chair. 'Mr Speaker, I have nothing more to say. These capitalists have not only subverted the free press of this country, they have also got some members of Parliament in their pockets.'

This time the treasury benches were on their feet. The speaker intervened. 'You have impugned the dignity of this house. This also will not go on record.'

'Sir, as a protest I will stage a walkout of the

House.' He strode out of the chamber. There was loud thumping of desks, boos and shouts of 'Good riddance. Stay out!'

Reports in next morning's papers added more bile to Nair's frayed temper. They did not report the unparliamentary expression used against him but gave every detail of how he had targeted his own minister, how he strode out in a huff and how his walkout was cheered. They devoted a lot of space to Nair having worked for Jai Bhagwan Enterprises and being elected to Parliament from a constituency heavily dominated by workers in his employer's mills. The implication was clear: Nair had betrayed the trust of a man to whom he owed all he had achieved in his life.

13

Ma Durgeshwari had something to tell Victor. In all
her life she had never felt as anxious about any
decision or its consequences as she did now. She had
not broached the subject on the yacht, nor for the
first few days after their return to Jai Bhagwan
Towers. But she could not put it off any longer.
Sitting with Victor in the balcony of his penthouse
after breakfast one morning, she told him. 'It is time
for me to return to the ashram.' Victor held her
hand. 'I have been selfish, Durgesh. You miss Sheroo.
We'll leave early next week and bring Sheroo with
us. I'll charter a plane to fly us all back. It should
have occurred to me—'

'You have not understood,' Durgeshwari

interrupted him. 'I am talking of returning to the ashram and never coming back.'

A frown appeared on Victor's brow. 'I don't understand. Can I ask why you are saying this now?'

'We were together because we gave each other happiness,' Durgeshwari explained quietly. 'We have had good times. Now we will only bring sorrow into each other's lives.'

'Don't be a child, Durgesh. You are talking of what those fools at the mill said. You should put that out of your mind, it will all blow over. You are overreacting.'

Durgeshwari put up a hand to stop him. 'It will not blow over. It was you who overreacted at the mill. I told you in the beginning that we must both be free, *hamare tumhare beech sambandh hoga, bandhan nahin* (we would have a relationship but we wouldn't be bound to each other). You have been behaving as a husband to a wife. You have jeopardized your reputation and unnecessarily made enemies. And we will always be in the public eye. There can be no freedom for us now. There will be no pleasure.'

Victor was distraught. What she was saying was true, but he could not accept it. 'I cannot imagine a life without you, Durgesh. The last two years have been the happiest period of my life. It is not easy for me to forget.'

'It won't be easy for me to forget either.' She took her time telling him the complete truth. She was silent for several minutes, then said, 'I am pregnant. It is your child.' Because she did not look up, she did not see the shock and confusion on Victor's face.

When he had recovered, he asked, 'How long has it been?'

'A month, I think. It was a mistake, but what is done is done.'

Victor said nothing. He felt trapped.

'I hope you won't ask me to get rid of it. That would be hatya (murder).'

'So what do we do now?' Victor asked, unable to keep the irritation out of his voice.

'No one should know. I can't afford that and nor can you. I have a place down South where I can go and spend some months in private. I can also leave the baby there. It will be safe and well looked after. Perhaps you can adopt it later.'

'Perhaps.' They both knew this was impractical.

A great sadness came over Victor. He pulled Durgeshwari to him and held her close. 'You will give me a few days, won't you? Bring Sheroo here. Just a few weeks. Make that your farewell gift to me.'

Durgeshwari put her arms around his neck.

They sat in silence for a long time. Neither had expected their unusual love story to end in this manner. Ma Durgeshwari was surprised by the tears in her eyes. After a while she turned to Victor. 'I think Bharati should know. I'd like to tell her myself.'

~

Bharati had suspected for long that the relationship between her father and Durgeshwari was not exactly that of a guru and a disciple. At first it had bothered her, for she was extremely possessive about her Papi. But she later came to terms with it as she realized that Durgeshwari made her father very happy. Victor, on his part, was careful not to upset his precious daughter, and always made it a point to spend time with her so that she wouldn't feel jealous or neglected in any way.

Ma Durgeshwari decided to speak to Bharati the very day she told Victor that she would leave him. She went to Bharati's office in Jai Bhagwan Towers late in the evening. Most of the staff had left by then. She shut the door behind her. Bharati sat across the table, facing her.

'I have something to tell you, Bharati,' Durgeshwari began. 'I'm pregnant. It's your father's

191

child.' She watched Bharati's face for any reaction. Bharati stared back impassively. She didn't say a word.

'Neither of us wanted this child, Bharati,' Durgeshwari continued. 'There's nothing to be done now. I cannot commit jeev hatya.'

'Don't be melodramatic,' Bharati replied icily. 'That won't be necessary.'

'I am planning to go away for a while. I shall have the baby and leave it where it will be cared for.'

Bharati interrupted: 'All I want is a guarantee that my father will never know where you leave the child. The press should never find out—absolutely no one must ever know. You must promise me that.'

Ma Durgeshwari said softly, 'You have my word. Your father cannot afford a scandal. You need not worry. I love him, you know.'

The meeting ended with the understanding that after a couple of weeks in Bombay with Sheroo, Ma Durgeshwari would return to her ashram for good. Bharati also insisted that the ashram be shifted to some other part of the country as soon as possible. She would bear the expense.

14

The 9th of June is an important date in the calendar of Bombayites. That day they expect the summer monsoons to break over their city. They watch the storm gauge at the base of Walkeshwar Road near the entrance of the Babul Nath temple to keep abreast of weather conditions. People get ready for the onset: On Chowpatty Sands bhelpuri sellers, fruit juice makers and paanwalas begin to move their stalls and gas lamps to their homes for safekeeping. At the Churchgate end hawkers appear on the sidewalks, selling gumboots and umbrellas. Coconut sellers disappear; their places are taken by sellers of chana and corn on the cob. Waters of the bay turn restless, fishing boats are towed away to safe moorings.

During Victor's lifetime, the last boat to disappear was *Jal Bharati*, whose silver-white presence on the dirty grey sea assured people that there was still some time for the monsoon to set in.

Black clouds roll in suddenly from the south-western horizon. They may be seen on the 3rd of June or the 7th or the 10th, but the 9th is the date fixed in people's minds. They may announce their arrival with lightning followed by claps of thunder. Or silently spread themselves across the sky and send down a gentle drizzle, before they open up their water sacks into a downpour. People rejoice; the sea loses its torpor. Angry waves build up in the bay and come surging towards the shore. They are checked by large cement tripods put up to halt their progress. They hurl themselves against the tripods; their spray rises many feet and splashes across Marine Drive drenching anyone or anything passing along it. Walkers disappear. Roads turn to rivers of muddy water. There are traffic jams all over the city's congested roads. For some days life in Bombay comes to a standstill.

Every year Victor looked forward to the advent of the monsoon in Bombay. But no sooner had it arrived than he began to tire of the incessant downpour. He had to stay in his penthouse. The only exercise he could take were yoga asanas. He did not have the same enthusiasm to make love to Durgeshwari. It was the same with Bharati and Swamiji: a lot of yoga but little appetite for anything else. And Sheroo became very grumpy. He ate well but had little exercise and farted a lot. Twice a day Ma Durgeshwari put on a raincoat and took him for a walk. He did not like being drenched and pleaded with his Ma to take him back. Then he stretched himself out on a sofa and snored.

However boring the monsoon made life in Bombay, Victor never missed his after-dinner walk on Marine Drive. Clad in a light raincoat and with an umbrella over his head he walked up to the Church Gate intersection and back. There were few people on the road. Later in the monsoon young Maratha boys appeared from nowhere, tied bells on their ankles and formed a ring holding each other around the waist. Then they danced in circles: *chhung, chung, chhung*. They rehearsed every night for the Gudi Padva festival in honour of Shri Ganesha when they would dance through the streets, leading processions carrying garishly painted idols of Ganapati to immerse in the sea now back to its pre-monsoon calm.

The year Durgeshwari decided to leave him, the

monsoon was particularly depressing for Victor. The dark clouds and cool breeze filled him with great longing and greater sadness. He began to feel old again. They did not make love. Though he had wanted her to stay for a few weeks with him before the final farewell, he found he was less unhappy when he was away from her. He spent his days in the office or being driven around the city in his car. In the evenings he had more than his regular quota of two drinks and went to bed early. He waited impatiently for the monsoon to end so he could get on his yacht again.

The monsoon departs with greater fanfare than at its arrival. There are huge bulbous clouds but they are waterless and white, not nimbus grey. They often run into each other with flashes of lightning followed by thunder. In the evening they catch the fire of the setting sun and light up the sky with an orange glow. But people know it is more noise and bluster without much rainy business. On Chowpatty Sands bhelpuri, paan, fruit juice and ice cream stalls are re-erected. Around Churchgate station, gum boots and umbrella sellers disappear. Sea waves no longer crash on tripods with the same fury nor spray Marine Drive with saline water. Fishing boats appear in the bay. In those long ago years the silver-white *Jal Bharati* reappeared in the sea soon after the fishing boats and the sight reassured Bombayites that the annadaata, the food provider, of thousands of families all over the country was still among them.

Victor was eager that year to leave his apartment and be on his yacht. He got daily reports from the dry docks of the work being done on it. When he was assured the yacht was as good and seaworthy as it was when he had acquired it, he had provisions sent aboard to last him at least a month. He announced his decision to his daughter, Ma Durgeshwari and Swamiji; he intended to be by himself for some time. He would leave on Saturday evening.

At 5 p.m. Victor left Jai Bhagwan Towers for the Gateway of India where *Jal Bharati* was moored with the gangway lowered to the steps of the gate. Marine Drive was crowded with walkers. The chauffeur turned left at the Churchgate intersection, past the High Court and University buildings, into the side road beyond the main entrance of Hotel Taj Mahal. There was a vast throng of humanity here; to Victor, impatient to escape the clamour and crowds of the big city, it seemed as if all of Bombay had spilled out onto the road. He asked the driver to pull up on the side; there was no way he could get to his yacht except by forcing his way through the crowd and through the massive Gateway, then down the steps to the gangway. Many people recognized his large Mercedes Benz. Many more recognized him as he stepped out of the car. Someone shouted out: '*Jai Bhagwan ki*', and dozens of voices replied: '*Jai.*' Victor waved a hand half-heartedly to acknowledge their acclaim; he needed to get away, out into the sea, so he could breathe again. He was a few yards from the Gateway when a volley of shots rang out. People ran in all directions, falling on each other. In the commotion, the car that had brought the killers to the scene of the crime sped away without anyone trying to stop it or taking down its number. By the time the chauffeur was able to get to his master, he was lying dead, drenched in his own blood.

Acknowledgements

Thanks to Janet Ward for going over the text and saying nasty things about it. My thanks also to Ravi Singh and Diya Kar Hazra for making it readable.